"Adventure? Romance? Steven's latest book has it all, and you'll be swept away on tides of excitement."

—GENE SPERRY, *Bookseller*

"A gripping romance set in a world of danger and betrayal. Intense and unforgettable—this story will keep you hooked from start to finish!"

—YOLA THORP, *Author*

"Steven James' *Swept Away* is a gripping tale of romance, mystery, and intrigue that kept me on the edge of my seat from start to finish. With vivid descriptions and well-developed characters, I was drawn into a world of suspense and surprises. This book is a must-read for anyone who loves a thrilling adventure, a touch of darkness, and a lot of heart."

—AYA, *Avid Reader*

"A thrilling romance novel that effortlessly weaves action, danger, and redemption. This book is a heartfelt journey where love triumphs over adversity."

—DAN WEAVER, *Author*

"Steven James' first foray into fiction finds fulsome fruition. Good pacing, engaging characters, vivid settings and a plot line that will keep you turning pages. Put it on your order list!"

—JORGE CARDOSO, *Education Dean*
Romancier Brazil, Portugal, Boston

"I read the first chapter and was immediately hooked. What a brilliant writer and creative talent. No better way to fill a beachy day. Keep those novels coming, Steven!"

—ROBERT LUCKOCK, *Journalist and Travel Writer*

A NOVEL

STEVEN JAMES

One Stop Publishing Group, LLC | www.OneStopPublishing.com

STOUGHTON MASSACHUSETTS

Swept Away: I'm Yours Forever
Steven James

Freedom Press Consulting
Cover and interior layout by twolineSTUDIO

Publisher: One Stop Publishing
              PO Box 474
              Stoughton, MA 02072
              Onestoppublishing.com

ISBN: 979-8-9856541-0-3

Dedication

For all the wonderful people who understand what love is.
Love is respect for everything and everyone!
Love surpasses religion, race, gender, ethnicity, and choice.

For all of you who believe in deep Romantic Love, including those who are with us now and those who have passed their spirits into all of us.
Love is the grace-filled way of honoring our ancestors and our children to come.

For all the wonderful people who helped me through my cancer journey—most especially my beloved wife Susan, my sons Dave and Phil, Michelle and Dave, my Stinky Brats, my doctors, my work connections, and my biking buddies.

Table of Contents

He Could Dance

Excited guests arrived at the gang plank to board the "Joys of Love" cruise ship at Miami's famed cruise dock in Florida. A cute young couple, first-time cruisers, quickly found the front of the line and snuck a kiss under the archway.

The day was young. The air was light. The weather held no promise of distress.

The young lady wore a white, tight-fitted top that pretended to cover her chest. Her pink, short skirt made the same attempt to cover her lower half. She reached on her tippy toes to extend to her anxious lover's lips for a magical kiss. The young man, himself quite handsome, brushed her red hair aside and reached around to pull her lithe body to his.

Handsomely attired staff in white jackets with brass-braided sleeves saluted and funneled their excited new patrons through the rose-covered archway to meet the ship's crew and hear the itinerary. Soft yellow lights lit up the couples' faces as the ship photographer snapped away.

One older single gentleman smiled at the young couple's magnetic attraction. *Perfect*, he thought as he snapped a picture with his cellphone. The couple's perfect entry lit up the archway and his hopes of romance, too.

The "Joys of Love" was one of six Mistresses of the Sea ships, owned and operated by the Arnoldo family. Royals from countries all over the world had been guests on the "Joys of Love." The proud staff poured personal pride into every detail of their guests' experiences.

Each of the function heads on board gave a simple presentation. Georgio, the top chef, with his gold ribbon-topped chef's hat, spoke of his love for unique cuisine. Georgio wasn't tall, and for sure, his robust figure was proof of his culinary skills. He proudly shared to all that he dedicated his life to the delicacies befitting queens and kings, an honor afforded him by the ship's owners and their incredible kitchen and staff. Marietta, his sous-chef, stood loyally by his side.

"The tongue is a temple for worship!" he often shouted to his team as he tasted each of their creations. He relentlessly drummed into his staff, "The tongue is the entry point to sensuality. To love itself!" These were the tenets of the great chefs that produced the delectable cuisine on the "Joys of Love."

His creations lit his guests' eyes and drew their attention as if a red carpet unrolled before them. Georgio's presentation of food shocked and pleased the eyes. His creations had to be exquisitely perfect. As far as Georgio was concerned, the ship's success hinged on his team's delicacies and exotic flair.

The guests' first sight of food included large, bright-orange carrot slivers piercing green olives centered in a hummus-red-pepper dip nestled in hand-poured pecorino romano parmesan bowls. In his heart, Georgio knew that where the ship was headed or how fast the ship travelled did not matter. The Casino and the shops carried great products, but that didn't matter, either.

"Pshaw," uttered Georgio in faux disgust. "Those are for fools." His department, *his* work, he knew beyond any doubt was the center of life itself on board.

As she listened to Georgio, Tina had to agree. She was tickled by the idea of sensual food. Her mind drifted off to thoughts of chocolate covered strawberries. She remembered her romantic young lover from college who insisted on positioning strawberries in a drizzled line of chocolate syrup from her cleavage to her belly button. He gently lined them up before he licked them off of her one at a time. She shivered inside at the thought.

She forgot his name, but not those sensual moments. It was such a shame he had disappeared. Tina thought they had a bond. She couldn't even remember why he left so suddenly. *Did she break it off, or did he?* Tina was ready to put the past behind her and wistfully envisioned exotic moments to come on her first single's cruise. She couldn't wait to find the pool, put on one of her new bathing suits, and release herself to the sun and whatever adventures awaited her.

Next to speak was Sheila. Sheila, in her thirties, was the activities director for the cruise. "I promise each of you that you'll all get a chance for love. That's right. That's a promise." Sheila was so upbeat—maybe too upbeat. That was one hell of a promise. For whom? Certainly not everyone. Tina listened to Sheila and rolled her eyes.

Tina went so far as to label what she heard. *It's all a lie*, she thought as she listened. Tina's negative side pushed even harder. *That's not happening.* But she fought with herself to leave a window, a tiny porthole, an entry open for love—maybe even a lover.

Really Sheila, Tina thought to herself. *Everyone will find the love of their life? That's bold. Especially for me.*

Tina had her heart broken enough times that she had to work hard not to hate men—not all men of course, not her dad or her brothers. But a good portion of the men she encountered came with unfaithful broken promises. She tucked away the hopes of a dream man in a secret place she wouldn't share with anyone. Tina believed that place would never see the light of day.

The men in line with Tina heard Sheila's speech and her siren call. Among them was Ricky, a Latin American engineer from Ecuador in his late twenties. He looked out to sea and sighed. Ricky was recently jilted by his girlfriend who happened to liberate him by way of his best friend. It wasn't pretty. Ricky needed a reset. He could smell the salt and feel the moisture of the ocean air as he stood on the upper deck overlooking the crystal-clear waters of the Pacific.

The Arnoldos were an old, Italian family that had invested millions in the romance market. They owned jewelry stores, a publishing house with several small magazines, and several vineyards in Italy. In the Mistresses of the Seas strategy room, their leadership team envisioned people like Tina and Ricky when they created their ads and wrote their brochures.

"Singles," the ads called out. "Come for fun and sun and leave with your match made in heaven."

The guests had high hopes and were eager to explore the ship. The long, frustrating lines in the Miami heat took its toll. Whether they were newbies on their first cruise or experienced "cruisers," the whole group descended on the staff with questions.

"Where are the free drinks?" one beer-bellied guest shouted.

The next bellowed out, "Where is the bar?"

Another asked, "Where is the highest pool deck?"

The questions fired out at a fever pitch and excited the normally placid rule-followers.

They all raced right by the neatly attired staff, and mostly ignored the neat desks with last name indicators and guest packets.

They were on a mission. Like children running into Disneyland, the guests poured themselves onto the decks, asking questions and scurrying about.

"How about that casino?!"

"Excuse me sir, can I get a Rum Swizzle? I'm thirsty as hell!"

It was mayhem, albeit somewhat controlled. The staff looked at each other in bemused bewilderment. The same scenes played out on each cruise. They had seen this before, but this crowd was especially boisterous. Perhaps it was the hot, beaming sun. One staff member knew better.

Flora May knew the date and the alignment of the stars. January 11, every year, presented its own opportunities and challenges. Her fortune-telling craft allowed her greater insight than the others. She knew there were angels performing and a devil to stop, too.

Marietta nodded calmly at the passers-by. She knew she'd learn their preferences, the exact way to steal their hearts, the old-fashioned way—treasures of the palate, plated to perfection, and delivered sensually with love.

Making her way onto the ship and standing in line to receive her cabin key, Tina felt hot, annoyed, and uncomfortable in her black leggings and fitted running top. She knew exactly what she wanted—a refreshing swim in one of the pools she'd seen in the brochure. She raced to the mezzanine deck. She had to be the first into that pool. She was "Type A" for sure, even on vacation.

Tina quickly found a changing room, threw off her travel clothes and slipped into the bottom of her black bikini she had tucked into her travel bag. She turned away from the mirror, looked over her shoulder to check the fit, and gave herself a double, tongue-click and a wink. It was the classic tease she dished to get men's attention at bars, especially when other women weren't looking. It worked one hundred percent of the time. She grabbed her top, fastened it in the front, spun it around quickly, adjusted her cups, and was off to the pool. She loved to be first—at everything. She was brash, maybe too confident, and competitive. After weeks strapped into the rowing machine, followed by countless hours on the Peloton bike, she had every right to be sure of herself and her body.

Just before Tina went into the pool, she sent a telepathic message to Sheila. *I'm holding you to your promises of love.*

She loved that she was the first one in the pool. She dove in barely making a splash, dolphin-kicking underwater to the end of the pool. When she came up, she could taste the salt in the air. The water was cool and soft on her skin. Tina wondered if they pumped the water directly from the ocean. It was so refreshing.

Tina had an edge to her. When she contemplated the cruise, she hadn't been in a meaningful relationship in quite a while. Men had been a punishing waste of time since her last boyfriend decided to move overseas to get a degree in "whatever." He liked dogs; she liked cats. He liked science; she liked sports. She lost interest in him, as he had lost interest in her. She hoped this cruise—a single's cruise—would provide the spark she needed, and maybe the love interest she wanted.

After taking in a bit of the ship's amenities, Ricky made his way to his cabin. He opened B-18 and scanned the room. A sliver of light drew him like a magnet to the porthole-sized window in his room. The sun's rays bounced off the water drawing his gaze directly to a figure floating gracefully in the deep end of the pool. He had paid the premium to get a bigger room with an outside deck. B-18 also had a birds-eye view of the mezzanine pool. Ricky came out onto the upper deck overlooking the pool to get a better look.

It was a woman. Her water and sun-drenched body entranced him. Long, silky, dirty-blonde, hair outlined the perfect curvatures of her face. He was sure she must be a model. She was stunning. Her skin was radiant. Her high cheekbones glistened in the sun. Her chin was strong with a defiant look, yet her features gave way to soft eyes. He was too far away to see if she had blue eyes, but since she had just become his dream woman, he knew that was their color.

The ship had left port several hours earlier. Standing outside his room staring down at the pool, shirtless and running his hands through his brown chest hair, Ricky couldn't wait to meet this woman swimming in the pool below. He continued to watch her as she rolled off her back in the water and seductively made her way to the shallow end of the pool. Her long, athletically defined legs beckoned him as she stepped onto the ladder. She made her way up the ladder like an angelic being, barely touching the rungs. Ricky was hooked. She looked as though she were floating above the deck as she walked. Droplets of water brilliantly reflected like diamonds on her perfectly sculpted body.

Ricky's heart beat rapidly. He was mesmerized by her beauty. An overwhelming desire to be close to her washed over him like a tidal wave.

He noticed he wasn't the only one focused on this goddess of a woman. Three men stood behind her by the pool and watched her every step with sheepish boy-like grins on their faces. Her hips moved as if propelled by music when she walked.

This woman captivated their attention. Ricky couldn't tell if she knew that all eyes were on her. As she made her way up the ladder, they stared at her black string bikini perfectly fit on her svelte body.

Ricky felt his body swell with a feeling he hadn't had in months, or was it a year? *Damn*, he thought, *it had been a long time.*

As she moved up the ladder, each leg whispered her strength and called for muscles like hers to entangle them.

Look at this, boys.

She took a few steps to the lounge chair where she had positioned her things and slowly bent over for her towel. She dabbed her face and smoothed out the lines of her bikini.

With the same graceful movements, she bent over and dried her lower body. She slowly dried each foot, each calf, and finally made her way up her perfectly toned thighs to her flat stomach and finally to her perky breasts. By now, the four men weren't the only spectators to this towel-dry event. Her routine had spawned interest from all corners of the pool area, the bar, and from high above. Her cleavage demanded to be watched, especially by Ricky's eyes.

As the afternoon wind blew lightly over her face, short wisps of hair crossed back and forth over her eyes—*blue diamonds in the sand*, Ricky hoped.

Dry and taut, Tina slipped on a sheer cover up and made her way to the poolside bar. She knew exactly what she wanted—Sex on the Beach, extra ice.

Ricky could see that even the bartender, Raoul, was taken by her beauty. He fumbled about a bit before preparing her drink. With a shaky hand, he placed the refreshing drink on the bar and topped it with a slice of fresh pineapple and a colorful umbrella. Ricky's mouth watered.

"Thank you," said Tina as she took a sip followed by a deep sigh of total relaxation. *This is exactly what I needed*, she thought.

Halfway through her drink and feeling quite free, Tina stood up and began to sway to the music on the pool deck. She moved back and forth, sensually arching her back. She tilted her head back, closed her eyes, and allowed herself to become completely lost in the moment. She dreamed of a special someone with more free-feeling moments like this on the cruise.

The men behind her at the pool looked at each other. She had swagger they had only dreamed about. Tina quickly became a contest. The guy with the dark black hair said, "Those legs . . . she must be a runner."

The thin blonde guy said, "No. She's a cyclist. I would know those leg muscles anywhere."

The third, a French guy wearing a tiny, black bathing suit, had been studying her since she climbed out of the pool. "No, she's a rower. Her shoulder blades are sculpted like a girl I dated in Paris." Tina's shoulders matched his memories exactly. He could always remember a woman after he made love to her.

They *all* wanted her. Her tight body and enchanting face held their eyes as if in a sorcerer's trance.

Tina finished her drink, ordered another, and made her way back to her lounge chair. She slowly removed the sheer cover up and positioned herself on her chair.

She reached into her bag and pulled out a bottle of tanning oil.

Damn, Ricky thought. *This little show is like ripping through a playboy book just to see the pictures.* He couldn't wait to get to the next scene. She squeezed the bottle over each leg, leaving a trail of oil to be massaged into her already lightly-bronzed skin.

Another squeeze and the bottle slipped out of her hand. Was that intentional? A pool attendant who had been watching her intently raced to grab the bottle for her. She smiled innocently and thanked him. Sweat covered his face as he stammered, "*De nada.*"

She took the bottle from his outstretched hand, threw him a "thank you" smile, and began to rub the oil on her chest, her fingers slipping in and out of her slinky black suit. If she had asked for volunteers, there would have been a stampede.

Tina wasn't the girl they all hoped she was. She was far more. They wanted her beauty and her body. She knew men dreamed of her as a happy-go-lucky, jump-in-the sack, and please-me girl. Their dreams about her weren't close. She wasn't jumping in the sack for any of them. Tear down that image. She was looking for so much more. It would take a very special man to lower her guard and open her heart, let alone make her willing to hop in bed.

Did any of these guys have what she wanted? What she needed? Did they have what it takes? She hoped to find out.

There had to be someone smart and loyal out there even if it meant she had to travel the seven seas to find him. Tina wasn't just looking for any guy. She had been there, done that. She wanted someone intriguing, funny, thoughtful, successful, and ambitious. If he happened to be handsome with a strong athletic build, she wouldn't complain.

She thought back to the life she left behind and reminded herself, *Insurance work is so boring.* Day after day she performed exactly the same routines but on different properties. She was tired of the monotony. She longed for overdue changes in her job *and* her personal life.

She wanted to find a man who would see her beauty from the inside out, not the outside in. It was easy for her to get her way with men. All she had to do was bat her long eyelashes, flash her beautiful smile, and be flirtatious and light-hearted. Her physical features attracted them all. She wanted this trip to be different. She wanted to meet someone with depth, not someone out for a quick encounter. Tina wanted the real deal. She wanted a man who "got her." Deep down, she longed for a man who would appreciate her for her inner beauty and treat her with love and respect.

Studying her from afar in his room, Ricky realized it was serious now. He had to meet her. *Hell, it's fair game. It's a single's cruise,* he thought to himself. His porthole had beamed him into the contest. He left his room and walked with confidence up to the bar. He ordered a gin and tonic, turned to her and smiled.

Tina didn't notice him. His heart sank to his feet. He felt like taking his drink back to his room, but he forced himself to stay. The whole reason he was on this cruise was to get over his insecurities around dating women. He forced himself to sit patiently and wait for a second chance to engage her.

She had four interested suitors now, and the cruise had just begun. The bartender, Raoul, felt like he had to protect this gorgeous woman. Maybe she didn't need him, but he'd keep an eye on her. He remembered his promise to his mother to protect women. It wasn't just because it was his job to look after the single women on the cruise, and not just because her perfectly sculpted body made him feel like a young, schoolboy; it was a duty that would define him for life. On top of that, he liked Tina at his bar. One look and she made him smile. Beautiful women like Tina were good for business. They always drew a crowd.

Ricky watched Tina from across the bar. This girl was electric. Her bouncy walk screamed to everyone that she was special. He wondered if she could dance?

Tina finished her drink and sauntered back to the bar. Ricky swung in over her shoulder, "Can I buy you a drink, sweetheart?"

Should she be a smart-ass and tell him she wasn't interested? A quick "No thanks" could do it. Her first impression was that he was a player. She thought about saying, "I know what you're up to. The drinks are free. Remember?" Instead, she decided to be nice and kept quiet. It would turn out to be a good decision.

The thin blonde guy from the pool came over and quickly complimented her, "Nice suit, cutie."

Wrong approach, buster. She smirked but didn't reply. That sent him away.

Rhythmic reggae music floated through the speakers on the pool deck. A steady beat pounded. She loved to dance. She hoped one of the guys would ask her to dance. Ricky took a chance and asked, "How about a dance?"

Relieved that at least one of the men would step up, she replied, "Oh yeah, sure."

Let's see if this guy can dance, Tina thought. *Maybe he can make this little contest interesting.* Oh yes, she knew this was a contest and *she* was the prize.

The answer came quickly. Ricky grabbed her hand, felt her rhythm by her touch, led her across the tiny dance floor, and spun her around. His gyrating hips could barely contain him. She was having trouble containing herself.

Now that's what I'm talking about.

Her heart pounded from the pace. She was breathless. Sweat rolled down her neck onto her breasts.

This man can dance, she thought as she tilted her head back and lost herself in the music. she allowed herself to wonder . . .

What else can he do?

A Mother's Influence

Raoul, the bartender, came from Brazil. His mother, Marietta, had worked the cruise lines out of Rio De Janeiro for decades. As a little boy, Raoul was saddened each time the ship embarked because he knew it was there to take his mother away for months at a time. While his mother was away, he got to play futbol with his cousins and even though his aunts and uncles took good care of him, he would have traded all the fun in the world to have his mother home with him.

Months later, when she returned, she'd tell him, "Buff up, Raoul. Make yourself pretty for the ladies. You will protect me and the pretty ladies. Eventually you will join me, and the ships will take us to see all over the world."

Marietta taught Raoul to be a good man, caring and aware of his family and the women around him. He was protective of them all, especially his sisters.

Throughout his childhood, Raoul and his mother enjoyed their time together. They loved to dance in the kitchen when she cooked. She would say, "Move those hips my little one. Smile for the girls."

She also taught him respect. He knew from a very early age never to touch a lady without her permission. Marietta taught him to look out for all women and made him promise he wouldn't allow other men to touch them either, without permission. He took this promise very seriously.

His aunts doted on Raoul when his mother was away. Marietta rewarded his aunts with gifts from faraway places like St. Maarten, England, Italy, Antilles, Netherlands, and so many more beautiful and exotic locations. She would enjoy her days off the ship shopping in local stores, gathering gifts to bring home to Raoul, his sisters, and the family. She loved her job and the freedoms it afforded her. She was proud of the life she had built for herself and Raoul.

Raoul grew to stand every bit of six feet tall. He had listened to his mother and found the weight rooms and boxing parlors when she was away. He didn't know his father, but he got his significant frame from him. In his late teen years, he found himself bulking up to 215 pounds of pure muscle. He was a natural boxer with a strong jab and an overpowering right hook. He had an impressive string of knock-outs in Rio's amateur circle, but his heart wasn't really in it.

His mother always said, "Be a lover, not a fighter." Fighting wasn't in his nature.

As his size and confidence grew, he learned that he didn't have to fight—but he knew how.

His brown eyes searched detective-like when he was near strangers. He quickly assessed friends, foes, and threats. With a sharply-pressed, white, short-sleeve collar shirt on, muscles protruding from his elbow to his shoulder, Raoul was an impressive figure—both to men and women.

On board the ship, his crisp uniform with pins on the lapel gave him an opportunity to exhibit a bit of swagger. When he walked into a crowd, people separated to let him through. The girls melted at how handsome he was. The guys gave way because they didn't want to bump into his substantial frame.

When Raoul wasn't in his uniform, he preferred designer clothes which he purchased at knock-off shops in New York. Occasionally he would throw on a Yankees baseball hat. It did not alter how he was dressed, Raoul emitted masculinity and power in a way that people responded to.

For Raoul's mother, Marietta, it was tough being on the cruise. She did it for the money. Money didn't come easy in Rio. Marietta was a cook. A damn good cook. And she was damned good looking back in the day. Over the years she worked her way to the top of the line. She knew the Captain, and how he liked his steak—nearly raw, with just a light sear. She traded favors with other members of the staff, and she always got what she needed.

Raoul worked his way from dishwasher to busboy to bartender. The Captain kept an eye on Raoul. He put him in the right places to grow his influence on the ship. Marietta's favors were worth his time for the boy. It was easy to get ahead with favors and special treatment. On board the ship, that's how things were done and everyone knew it.

Raoul was a quick study. He was always respectful. Raoul would see the Captain, fix his collar, and immediately look into his eyes and issue a respectful, "Captain, Sir!" The Captain would have nothing less on *his* ship. Watching from above at his station, he exhaled comfortably as he watched Raoul hustle drinks to patrons at the pool bar as if the boy had tended bar his whole life. Raoul "owned" the bar. He was an absolute natural, and his customers were drawn to him. It was a good assignment for the young man. He was great at managing the crowds of demanding customers, and he was especially good with the ladies. There were plenty of tips for a man with his looks and skillset.

Raoul could make great small talk, anything from sports to relationships to the weather. He had a charming way of digging deeper into real issues. His charisma made him a perfect bartender. Raoul understood that people have strong opinions, and most just want someone to listen to them—to feel seen and heard. Raoul could make anyone feel important. It wasn't an act. In his mind the cruise's clientele were *his customers and were very important.* His mother had taught him well.

Nothing could get by him when he was behind the bar. When people whispered their secrets, Raoul could hear them as if he had sonar. And from his elevated platform, he could see everything even as he ducked under the wine racks to catch eye contact with customers. He was very perceptive and could feel when trouble might be brewing. Raoul didn't like the looks of the three men who had followed the cute, black-bikini-clad girl up to his bar. It wasn't unusual for women in nice bathing suits to be at his bar, but this girl had some sort of magnetic attraction. The guys were all over her every step, and he didn't like it.

Raoul watched the three men carefully. The blonde guy had a nervous look to him—his eyes were darting around quickly, and his right hand shook with a nervous twitch. He seemed on edge. Raoul made a mental note to keep a close eye on him.

As he circled the bar checking in with those who had a few too many, and others who were just getting started, he thought he saw the blonde guy's right hand hover above the beautiful woman's drink. His instincts were right. He had seen this before—men who didn't stand a chance otherwise trying to take advantage of beautiful women. He was sure he saw the blonde guy drop something in her drink.

Not on Raoul's watch.

Raoul quickly made another Sex on the Beach and set it aside. He swooped over to where the woman's drink was and "clumsily" spilled her drink before she could take another sip. It didn't bother him one bit to play the fool if it meant keeping a customer, especially a woman, safe.

"I'm so sorry, Miss. I'll get you another."

Raoul quickly cleaned up the drink, grabbed the pre-made one, and set it down with an expressive smile.

"Here you go, Miss." He turned away from her, eyeing the blonde guy, "May I have your name, Miss?"

"My name is Theresa, but you can call me Tina."

"That's lovely, Miss Tina."

He walked to where the blonde guy stood at the bar. Raoul towered over him. Raoul leaned toward the blonde guy and made sure

Tina could not see what he was about to do. Raoul grabbed the guy's ear and pinched it hard enough to make him wince. Raoul's muscled frame said, *don't fuck with me asshole*, but he had another message that he whispered in the guy's quickly swollen ear: "I swear on my mother's grave, I will hunt you down and rip your ear off your head if you ever touch that lady or so much as look at her again or anyone else at my bar. You are tired now, aren't you?"

The thin blonde guy stammered, "Hey guys, I'm out of here. Gotta hit the hay."

Tina looked confused. She thought to herself, *what just happened?* Maybe I'll see him tomorrow. Maybe not.

One of the other two guys yelled, "Dude, where are you going? We are just getting started. This bar is freakin' awesome!"

The blonde guy turned back. His face turned rash-red. He looked more agitated than before.

"Fuck you! I'm out of here. I'm checking out another bar!"

Tina was shocked. She wasn't sure the guys who argued were friends, but they didn't seem like they were arch enemies when they were jostling around in the pool. She thought to herself, *life gets stranger by the day*. She chocked it up to too much drinking after the long lines. She wondered why the red-faced guy was so pissed.

She would soon find out.

Room Upgrade

Tina never saw the blonde guy again. There was something odd about the guy. She had a sixth sense about him—like she had dodged a bullet. Still, she was curious about him. She wondered why she had that funny feeling. *Why do I feel so strangely about him?* Tina wasn't interested in *any* man. There were lots of men on the cruise. She wanted the "right man." The blonde guy probably didn't deserve a bit of her attention. He wasn't the *one* and she knew it right away.

Tina's mom always said, "You'll know the *one*." After a few years of being single and seeing her close friends get married before her, Tina wasn't as sure of her mom's advice. But Tina was sure she'd get the signals inside herself when the one for her showed himself in her life. Signs were a big thing for Tina. She would often seek the advice of fortune tellers when she had questions she could not answer herself. She hoped she would find those signs on this singles cruise. There would be plenty of guys for her to think about.

When they first boarded the ship, Tina was one of the smart ones who stopped at the welcome tables instead of rushing through to the bar. She grabbed her room packet after she went through the rose-covered archway. Nicely adorned, the packet came with a velvet-red, heart-shaped box of chocolates. She pulled the white plastic key out of the packet and went to room C-111 to settle in and unpack.

She opened the door to a balcony suite with a view of the ocean. She was ecstatic. She was sure she had chosen an inside room to save some money. She hoped there wasn't a mistake. The packet and the room matched. Tina James—Room C-111.

Was this a sign?

The view was beautiful, and the room was amazing! The sconces in the room highlighted a soothing aqua blue paint on the walls. The carpet below was soft and soothing to her tired feet. There were several small paintings with sunsets on one side of the room, and sunrises on the other side.

It was perfect.

Each of the paintings showed the ocean from a different angle. One of the paintings held the water in the foreground as if in a crystal-clear chalice with the sun beaming through the water. A second painting on the opposite wall showed the sun streaking through clouds and dancing across small, frosted, wind-driven wave tops.

She sat for a minute on the edge of the bed to take it all in. She imagined herself on a small boat bobbing in the picturesque waters surrounding the ship with a new-found lover. Their little boat bounced gently on the waves. Fish danced up and out of the water, then playfully darted in and out with shiny, silver streaks breaking left and right. Her lover looked deep into her blue eyes, quietly taking her in. He didn't try to break her stare. He was absolutely mesmerized by her.

Tina was lost in her daydream. An involuntary yawn pulled her attention back to reality. After her quick dip in the pool and the episode at the bar, Tina needed to refresh. She thought about turning in for the night. It had been a long first day and the sun and drinks had left her drowsy.

The bed had a fluffy, silky comforter with a pink and yellow flower print on it. It reminded her of her favorite comforter back home. Still on the edge of the bed dreaming of possibilities, she reached for a pillow to support her shoulders. In an instant she was asleep.

Tina woke the next morning to a knock at her door.

"Is everything in order with your room, ma'am?" a crew member asked from outside the door.

"Why, yes, I love it," she said. But in the back of her mind, she wondered about the upgrade. She struggled in her mind about whether she should ask.

"Good, I'm so glad everything is to your liking" the crew member responded. "We encourage you to take advantage of our complimentary packages. The brochures are on your night table."

"Thank you," she responded, sleepily.

It took her a few more minutes to wake up, but eventually curiosity won her over. She sat up and glanced to her side. On her nightstand was a complimentary pass for a massage.

What the hell. I'll check out the spa, she thought. *You only live once.*

She tossed on her morning sweatshirt, skipped the bra, ran a brush through her long, silky, blond hair and ran down to one of the ship's coffee shops for a quick, to-go cup of energy.

Great! She thought. *They have Columbian and a few chocolate sticks to drop in—my favorite.*

On her way back she saw Raoul preparing his pool bar station for the day. *What was it about him? Somehow she knew she could trust him. Maybe more than that . . .?*

In his typical cruise-friendly way, Raoul looked up and greeted her, "Good morning, Miss Tina. What's on your ticket today?"

"I'm thinking of that complimentary massage," Tina answered.

"That's a great idea, Miss Tina!"

Raoul beckoned her over. "I've got a friend in the spa. He is a master masseuse. His name is Jawon."

Whispering now, "He'll take you right to the edge. But not over the line."

Tina smiled. Raoul smiled back and said, "Jawon and I have an agreement. I send him nice ladies. He knows how I am. He'll never, ever go too far, or he'll answer to me."

Raoul tightened his chest muscles, cocked his head to the side, winked, and gave her a shiny-tooth grin. "Capiche, Miss Tina? Now go and have fun—and tell him I sent you."

She couldn't help herself. She blushed. *What was that all about?* She sifted through the conversation in her mind, then lifted her elbow and with her index finger gave Raoul an imaginary tip of her hat, along with a wide, beaming smile.

She felt her stomach get warm. *Where was this heading?*

Tina wanted to explore the ship, but for now, she knew exactly where she was going. She found herself practically running up the stairs to get a better view of the ocean.

At the top of the stairs, the ocean view was spectacular. She ran to the edge rails and pressed herself just over the top rail. She lifted her heels slightly off the deck and leaned forward onto her toes as a soft breeze lifted her hair off her shoulders. It was exhilarating. Tina lived in the unbridled bliss of the moment. She thought, *Just this once, no planning. Just live in the moment!*

Behind her, dishes fell and shattered. She jumped. It made her think, even second guess, *Was this a sign?*

The noise pulled her from her private, fun, tip-toe moment. She turned around quickly. A reluctant waiter winced and bent over to clean the mess.

Had he been watching her?

She hoped not. And then she thought again.

Why should I care if someone sees me enjoying myself in the breeze? Let them watch. No one could know what I'm thinking. And who cares if they did!

She looked at the waiter's face. She couldn't bring herself to just step over the cracked dishes. Together they quickly cleared the mess before anyone noticed.

"What's your name?" she asked.

"Linau," he said.

"Linau?" She asked with curiosity.

"Yes, Miss. Please don't tell anyone, Miss . . ."

"Don't worry. It will be our secret. I'm Tina," she said, as she turned away.

Tina was happy to help. It was in her DNA. Behind Linau, she saw a sign for the "High View" lounge. Even though the massage idea tickled her, she decided to check out the food in the "High View" first. It was one of many bars and lounges that the ship had on almost every deck. She popped in and asked for a menu.

The bartender was a slightly balding older gentleman. Pierre came loaded with a cheerful disposition. Tina looked for vegetarian options and came across baked avocado shells with pistachio nuts and eggs. It sounded delicious.

She asked Pierre, "How are the avocado eggs?"

"C'est magnifique," said Pierre with a grin, "You will love them like the moon loves the stars."

She couldn't help but giggle. Pierre was quite funny with his splashy commentary. She liked him instantly. She knew she'd come back to the "High View."

"A coffee while you wait?"

"Yes, that would be nice. And a chocolate stick, please?" asked Tina.

Pierre slipped around the corner and returned with her coffee and two foil-wrapped milk chocolate sticks. She sipped the delicious coffee, gazed out at the horizon, relaxing until the eggs came.

The over-easy eggs were nestled in two perfectly ripe, avocado half-shells. Paprika, sea salt, pistachio bits, and freshly ground black pepper were sprinkled over the top with a parsley garnish. There were two tiny, thumb-sized French croissants on each side of the eggs. Thin slices of cantaloupe beautifully trimmed the plate. She wanted to pinch herself.

Almost too beautiful to eat, she thought.

The warm croissants were fresh enough to fall apart the minute they touched her tongue. She could taste a hint of cinnamon and butter. She followed up the croissants with a slice of the sweetest cantaloupe she had ever tasted.

Everything was perfect! She was in heaven. *What a terrific first meal*, she thought as she remembered Georgio's speech about the food. He wasn't kidding. The food on the "Joys of Love" was a sweet, inviting kiss to the tongue.

After eating every delicious bite, Tina sat, lost in the breathtaking views of the ocean. She had never felt so relaxed. The magic of the ship was getting to her as she felt her shoulders release and the tension in her back melt away.

She let herself daydream about her upcoming massage.

4

A Massage with Strawberries

After her delightful breakfast and time relaxing and staring out into the vast ocean, Tina made her way to the spa. When she arrived, she was greeted by a beautiful Asian woman named Rose. "Welcome, we are so glad to have you at the spa this morning." She offered Tina a cold glass of bubbly champagne and two perfectly dipped, chocolate-covered strawberries. "Thank you. What a treat," she said as she sipped the sweet champagne.

A tall, handsome, young, male assistant met her and led her into a dimly lit interior room. A cushioned bed with puffy pillows and a head rest was positioned in the middle of the room along with a small chair on four wheels for the masseuse. Several beautiful African animal carvings made from dark wood adorned the walls. The room was warm. Aromas of vanilla and lavender filled the air. She could feel herself becoming more and more excited.

The assistant handed her a small, pink silk robe and directed her, "You can undress here and put your things on the shelves." There were several old, Victorian-style, brass hangers under the shelves to hang her clothes.

"After you undress, you can lie face down on the massage table. It is heated to the perfect temperature, and I believe you will find it very comfortable," the assistant assured her.

"Take your time Miss Tina. Jawon, your masseuse, will be in shortly. "Thank you," Tina said shyly.

The room had a large mirror against one wall. Tina liked mirrors. As a child she would dance around in her bedroom in front of mirrors. As an adult, she loved how mirrors brought in light and made rooms look bigger and more cheerful.

Tina unzipped her pink shorts and effortlessly slid out of them, exposing her leopard thong underwear. She rubbed herself and felt guilty about her own playful touch in the mirror.

What are you worried about? she said to herself. *Why not feel good about looking good and getting a massage?*

She was tired of reigning herself in. She was going to enjoy this massage. Tina slowly undressed, consciously brushing her left nipple. Deep breath.

How much touching will this massage include? she wondered to herself. *Face down? How about my bottom?* Her mind was racing.

She sighed to herself, trying to let go and relax into this experience.

Tina took one last look at her naked body in the mirror and then slid into the massage table. It felt amazing. She took a few deep breaths and could feel every muscle in her body relax against the warm table.

Jawon tapped lightly in the door.

"Come in," Tina said nervously.

In a deep, soothing voice he leaned close to her and whispered, "Are you ready for your massage, Miss Tina?"

Tina was so ready she thought of blurting out, "Fuck yes. I'm ready!" The good girl in Tina held in that crazy but truthful voice as she stammered, "I'm a lit . . . little embarrassed."

"Miss Tina, do you have any tender spots?"

Her mind ricocheted in all the right and the wrong places. *What was he asking?* her mind raced.

Jawon went on to say, "I'll take care of you. Don't worry. Just pretend that your best friend is giving you the massage. Let the music relax you. I'm sure that you'll feel great at the end."

Tina hoped he was right.

Jawon moved slowly in everything he did. He had learned from years of giving massages that people—both men and women—interpreted fast movements as a threat. He wanted his clients to relax—no threats.

"So tell me, Miss Tina, have you had a massage before?"

Tina replied, "Only one or two. I have trouble with strangers touching me. It's a bit unsettling for me."

"I understand," replied Jawon. "I feel that way too, and I give massages for a living."

"Really?" she asked.

"Yes. It's not something people do every day. I certainly don't. Like yourself, I have to work. A good massage takes time. When I get a massage, I'm always comparing, so it's hard for me to relax. It's not like polishing an apple. It's more like how a cat learns to trust their owner. It's an inch-by-inch sort of thing. Don't you agree?"

"I guess so. I never thought about it that way," said Tina after giving Jawon's analogy a bit of thought.

Tina thought about her cats back home. At first, they were so jittery. She only won their trust after months of slowly pushing their dishes toward them with her foot. When she first got them, they didn't like her to bend over near them or they'd scurry away.

She was settling into the quiet ambiance of the room. The music did relax her. She thought to herself, *Jawon seems like a real sincere guy. He gets how scary a massage can be.*

Jawon placed a small stool at the edge of the massage table. "Are you ready to begin?" he asked gently. Tina tensed her muscles for a moment and then relaxed. "Yes, I'm ready," she said with a deep breath in and out. Her shoulders shivered.

Jawon reached into the warmer and pulled out a warm weighted blanket. He placed the blanket gently over the lower half of Tina's body. "This will help you relax even more," he said. He was right. The blanket felt like a warm hug.

Jawon started the massage at the base of Tina's neck slowly working the muscles of her shoulders between his large thumbs and forefingers on each side of her neck. He had a habit of making small talk with his clients to keep them relaxed. He asked Tina, "By the way, what do you do for work?"

Tina thought for a moment, *Does he really want to know, or is this part of the massage program?* She decided to be straightforward even if it didn't sound that way.

"I do many things. I work in the insurance industry part-time doing claims work. I also pick up a couple of hours at my local library, and I'm trying to break into the travel industry as a writer," shared Tina.

"Really? That's so interesting. A dual career—insurance and writing," said Jawon.

Tina responded, "Well, not exactly—I'm not exactly getting paid for writing yet. I've written a couple of articles for my local newspaper and one of my articles was accepted in a small travel magazine called 'Travel the World in Style.' Have you heard of it?" Tina asked.

"No. I haven't." replied Jawon.

Tina reassured him, "It's okay. It's not that well-known. Not many people have heard of it."

Jawon countered, "That sounds like a great way to get your foot in the door. Will you write about your adventures here on the 'Joys of Love?'"

"Yes, I hope so. I plan to keep a journal and hope to submit an article when I get back home," replied Tina.

Jawon wrinkled his brow and said, "Well in that case, I better do a really good job."

Tina smiled. In such a short time, they really hit it off. *It's funny how certain people just get along,* she thought to herself. *This might be one of those lucky encounters. Who would have thought I could get along with a cruise ship masseuse?*

Jawon slowly worked his way from the top of her shoulders down each arm to her wrists and hands. He was meticulous. He worked every muscle.

Tina felt limp by the time he worked his way back up to her shoulders.

Next, his strong fingers worked down her spine, slowly encircling each vertebrae. He continued his firm movements descending in a spine-tingling, slow movement toward the top of her buttocks. He made sure her back muscles released completely before moving on to her legs.

Jawon checked in with Tina. "How does your back feel now? I don't want to use too much force. To me, your upper back seems nice and relaxed now."

"Oh, yes. No problem. It feels great," replied Tina sleepily. He was an excellent masseuse. Jawon's strong but gentle touch, the smell of coconut oil and lavender, and warmth of the table were lulling her into deep relaxation.

"Good. I'm going to work on your legs next."

Jawon kneaded her powerful legs muscles back and forth. He couldn't help but notice how strong her legs were. He guessed she had done a considerable amount of biking or running. She had an impressive physique. His hands traveled from the inside of her knees up to her back side. His thumbs hinted toward her private area as he worked her upper thighs. Creating sexual tension wasn't his intention, but Tina certainly felt aroused by his hands sweeping up and down her legs.

She completely lost herself in the rest of the massage. Every care and worry she had faded away beneath Jawon's hands.

Tina was disappointed when Jawon finished her massage. It wasn't what she expected. She hadn't dreamed of enjoying it that much.

"Miss Tina, please take your time. You can lay here for a while and continue to relax. It was my pleasure to meet you," said Jawon as he placed his hand on the small of her back then slowly slid out the door.

It's over? Uhhh, she thought.

Tina could have stayed there all day with Jawon rubbing all one hundred and six bones of her body. That's the number of bones she remembered from her grade school health class. She had not been this relaxed in as long as she could remember. She didn't want the feeling to leave her. She got up from the table slowly again catching a glimpse of herself in the mirror. She was glowing.

She slipped into her clothing feeling like a new woman.

Rose came in and helped Tina gather her things. Tina grabbed her purse and a twenty-dollar bill. Rose walked Tina to the lobby of the spa where Jawon was waiting to tell her goodbye.

Tina handed Jawon the twenty-dollar tip. She hadn't seen him this clearly in the darkened massage room. *He was quite handsome.*

Jawon took the twenty and with a soft smile said, "Please come back and see us again, Miss Tina."

"I most certainly hope to," replied Tina. "Thank you so much for a wonderful morning."

Tina came out from the spa, looked up at the sun, and rolled her shoulders. *That was amazing!* she thought to herself. She decided to take a leisurely walk around the ship before heading back to her room. The sun felt warrm on her skin and face and the salt-tinged air was so refreshing. As she walked along, her body felt absolutely alive from Jawon's touch.

The fresh air was a reminder that she had taken strong steps toward the change in her life she wanted so dearly. She felt really great about herself for the first time in a long while. She didn't like to admit that she was disappointed in her life's direction. This cruise was a big step. She had made up her mind that she would have to create the change she wanted. So here she was, ready and willing . . ..

After a half-hour of exploring, she returned to her room. As she pulled her entry key card out of her purse, the French guy from the pool was coming toward her.

"What a pleasure to see you, Mademoiselle."

"Oh, hi," replied Tina.

"Would you like to have lunch?" he asked with high hopes and a boyish grin.

"Oh, how nice of you to ask," she responded. "I've just come from having a massage and a bit of a long walk. I need to freshen up. Could we make it another day?"

"Oh, how you pretty women love to disappoint us eager men. I didn't get your name?"

"It's Tina."

"Great, Tina." He started thinking about her body climbing the ladder out of the pool.

"Now that I know your cabin, perhaps I could stop by a little later?"

Whoa, whoa, whoa there, Frenchy, she thought to herself. "That won't be necessary" she replied with a soft grin. She added, "I'll find you when I'm ready."

There wasn't a signal to be had. She shut the door as the French guy was saying, "Have a great afternoon, doll."

5

Yoga on Deck

After dozing off a bit after her massage, Tina arose to the smell of the salt air from her cabin window. The day was still young. On her nightstand were the cruise activity brochures. Island hopping, jet skiing, dance lessons, singles meet-up, and yoga.

Yoga? That sounds really good, she thought to herself. Tina loved yoga. She was hoping to meet more spiritual types. The brochure said, "Singles, Meet Your Match." She knew that was a lie. She thought to herself, *You have to play along, Tina.*

Yoga was on the third deck out in the open air at the fore starboard side of the ship. She reminded herself that facing frontward in the direction the ship was sailing, starboard is the right side. It made her happy just to know the terminology. *Simple pleasures,* she thought to herself.

She took the main ship elevator from just outside her room up to the third deck. A young couple was heading in the same direction.

"Hi there," the man said with a jovial greeting. Tina smiled back. The woman asked, "Are you going up for yoga?"

Tina certainly looked yoga-ready with her tight-legged, hot-red striped yoga pants. Tina replied, "Yes. I'm excited to get some fresh air and good yoga karma."

"Have you done yoga before?" the woman asked.

"Well, yes," she replied. "But I'm not very good at it—especially the planks."

"I can't do those at all," laughed the woman.

The man proudly chirped, "I can do about a minute and a half." He readily took the opportunity to puff himself up in front of the ladies. He was an interesting looking fellow, sporting a handlebar mustache and a ponytail. English, Tina guessed from his accent.

The elevator door opened to the warmth of the golden sun. Yoga aspirants huddled in small groups waiting for instructions.

A smallish woman with blonde hair in a loose khaki outfit fiddled with a CD player on a table near a stack of chaise lounges.

Tina watched the pretty blonde as she moved across the deck in her direction and thought she detected frustration. "Hey," Tina said, "Need any help? I'm pretty good with audio stuff."

"Yes, please. I can't get my music to play."

"Let me have a look," replied Tina.

"That would be awesome."

In a minute, Tina found the loose connection, and sweet sounds of Trevor Hall filled the deck. Perfect yoga music.

"Oh, thank you so much! I'm Severina. You can call me Siv."

Siv peeled off her khaki outfit. She had a perfectly sculpted body. She looked like she might have been a ballet dancer. Tina was impressed.

Siv walked out on to the deck and announced the start of the class. "Hello, everyone. My name is Severina. I'll be your instructor today. Please call me Siv. I teach a type of yoga inspired by Kundalini yoga, which means we will be doing a soft, meditative style of stretch yoga. I'll try to make our moves clear and doable for everyone regardless of your yoga experience or fitness level. Please just follow along with my instructions and listen to your body.

Tina appreciated how thorough Siv was. She could tell she was a master yogi with much to teach her and the others in the class.

Siv began, "Don't push yourself too much. If it hurts, please stop. Yoga asks you to stretch your ligaments and increase the range of your muscles. Stretching must be gradual. If your joints hurt or your muscles feel extra tight, listen to your body, slow down, and be less aggressive. Only do the moves that support your body. Stretch only as far as you can incrementally. Remember to be gentle with yourself. Call me over and ask questions too. This isn't a boot camp. You are on a cruise. Relish in your great decision to be here—in the moment. Let's keep it light and fun."

Siv rolled out her purple yoga mat as she continued. The group followed her lead and began rolling out their colorful yoga mats.

Siv continued, "If you do stretch a bit too much and your feeling achy, we've got a great massage crew on board that you can see later in the day."

With a mischievous smile, Siv added, "Jawon and Rose can cure almost anything that's giving you trouble." The group smiled back. Tina nodded in approval. Jawon and Rose had healing powers for sure.

"For anyone who would like hot yoga or a faster pace, there is a second class in the afternoon. Our class will give you a nice mix of gentle stretches with relaxation to prepare you for a fun-filled day at sea."

Tina thought to herself again, *Siv is dynamite.* Tina couldn't wait for the class to start. Several of the guys near Tina were thinking the same thing—probably not just about the yoga though. She couldn't blame them. Siv was one *hot* yoga teacher—no one could argue that.

Siv continued, "There's a bin of foam blocks and towels near the table with the water." She pointed, "Make sure to hydrate. It's okay to stop during the class and grab a sip. If you need the bathroom, it's just around the corner on the port side. On the ship, we call a bathroom a 'head.'"

Siv pointed to the right. "Feel free to get your blocks and towels. We'll start in five minutes."

The soft beat of the music and Siv's gentle approach got everyone in the mood to relax. Most of the women had on attractive yoga leotards. The men had on bathing suits and shorts except for one tall thin man with a high and tight ponytail.

Siv spoke loudly as she addressed the group, "You are all going to be 'Siv's Yoga Army' for the rest of the cruise, so let's get some discipline here people."

The group looked at each other with uncertainty. Nervous giggles could be heard around the group.

"Space yourselves out a little more. Keep about a body's length between you and the next person, unless you are really tall, then you might need a little extra space."

The tall, ponytail guy wore a purple, see-through shift made of a very thin silk with a second layer of sheer white cotton. He took a position near Siv. After doing a round of reassurances around the deck, Siv came back to the front. She asked the ponytail guy to move a bit farther back to give her some space. He frowned and moved his mat a few inches away.

"I need a little more room," Siv urged gently.

No movement.

"More than that," Siv said firmly, tilting her head giving him the "stink eye," belying her strength in spite of her gentle approach.

Ponytail guy kicked his mat.

"Really?" Siv squinted her eyes as she stared him down. Siv was not the kind of woman one messed with. *Not my preferred mood setter*, Siv thought to herself. *Everybody is watching.*

Siv chalked it up to ponytail guy's ego and decided to use his mini-tantrum as a lesson for the group. Siv had handled many of these challenges with success. She just needed to keep her cool, continue her form, and let it play out. She reached down inside her peaceful place and thought positive thoughts, *I can use this to get the class started on the right foot.*

"Okay, then, Yoga is about relaxing. Let's all relax into our beginning poses."

"What's your name?" Siv asked the ponytail guy.

"Trinidad," he replied.

"Alright then, Trinidad, let's show the group how it's done. Try to leave room for a mat on all sides of your space."

Trinidad stepped back awkwardly and adjusted his mat a bit farther away.

The group riveted its attention to the pair at the front.

"Let's start with some gentle sun salutations. Stand at the top of your mats with your feet firmly planted."

Siv led by example as she walked to the front end of her mat.

"Feel the mat beneath your feet. Slowly feel each of your toes as they sink into the mat to help your balance. Next reach up to the sky with both hands. Imagine a strong cord stretching from your toes to your fingertips. Gently stretch that cord."

Siv demonstrated, stretching her long, lean body. Everyone could clearly see the defined muscles in her long legs. Her body was toned like a Greek goddess.

"Now let your hands swan dive down to your feet. Try to keep your breathing nice and even. Feel the warmth of the sun. Let's soak in every ray of the sun's energy together."

Just then Trinidad lost his balance. He reached out to prevent a fall. Nothing to grab. Siv, reached forward with her hand on Trinidad's back to prevent him from falling and embarrassing himself.

With grace and a gentle tone, Siv said to Trinidad, "Maybe being closer is better."

Everyone laughed.

Nicely done, Siv, thought Tina as she watched from farther back. Tina was on board with Siv's approach to yoga.

Siv continued, "Yoga is a time to relax. Let's keep our butt-checking to a minimum during our practice. You can do that at the pool."

The group laughed in appreciation of Siv's humor as they acknowledged the obvious. For most of them, men and women alike, they were guilty as charged. They loved Siv's sense of humor and easy way of being honest with them.

"For you pragmatic folks, yoga is a wonderful way to make things you do in everyday life easier, whether it's reaching to the top shelf in your kitchen cabinets for a box of cereal or bending over to pick up a spoon you dropped. Yoga will make all those movements easier. As you get older, your attention to your yoga practice will ease the aging process, too."

For the older members in the group, Siv's message was spot-on. Many of them recognized the need to get their bodies in better shape.

Siv went on, "Next, we'll do some core strengthening. Everyone, find your mat and take a seated position."

"Extend your legs like this," Siv demonstrated, as she quickly lowered herself to the mat and motioned them all to join. Siv noticed some members of the group struggled to get on their mats. She added, "If you were one of the late-night closers at the bar last night, the distance to the floor is probably painful. So move your mat near the rail. You can use the rails to get up and down."

The group laughed heartily. Siv's no-judgment zone made exercise fun.

She continued, "Once you've found your mat and are seated, reach toward your toes. Wherever you can comfortably reach is fine. It can be your knees, your shins, your ankles, it doesn't matter. Just stretch as much as you can. Remember to enjoy the sun too. Stretch and hold. One, two, three, hold, a few more seconds . . . and release. Feel the sun on your face."

Tina was enjoying Siv's direction and had no trouble reaching far past her toes. She was strong *and* flexible.

"Okay, now keep your left foot extended and bring your right foot in toward your body. Reach your left arm around and hug your knee. Extend your right arm behind you for support and lean back. Twist your upper body to the right and look behind you as far as you comfortably can. One, two, three, hold, a few seconds more . . . and release."

Siv could hear sighs and saw that each member was beginning to relax into the yoga practice. She smiled. She loved seeing people surrender to themselves.

"How is everybody feeling? Are you getting the kinks out?"

Several people in the group nodded and a few of them shouted out, "Good. Great! Keep going."

Siv continued, "Alright, switch legs. Extend your right foot and pull your left foot in toward your body. Reach your right arm around and hug your left knee. Twist your upper body to the left and look over your shoulder. Feel your neck muscles stretch gently. Don't go too far. Remember to listen to your body."

The room was warming up and everyone's stretches grew deeper.

"Next we'll do Chaturanga. Sometimes it's called a 'plank.' It's like a push-up that gets stuck in the 'up' position parallel to the ground. To get in position, first we'll get on all fours and then reach your right leg back. Next put your left leg back and press yourself up on your arms with your toes bent. Alright everyone, if your back is up to it, lift up and stay parallel to the ground. Tuck your tummies in and keep your butts low. Let's see how long we can hold our planks."

Less than a minute ticked off the clock. Siv let them off easy. It was the first day.

"Great job, everyone," Siv encouraged.

"Next we will stretch our backs in cobra pose. Allow your full body to make contact with the mat, push your hands hard into the mat and come up into cobra pose.

Siv demonstrated.

"Maybe close your eyes and see if you can feel chakra shivers in your spine. If you do, take a minute to enjoy that feeling. Some of you may even be able to help that energy travel through your shoulders. Don't worry if you don't feel it yet. Just relax as much as you can and enjoy the sun's energy."

Siv spoke slowly as she introduced more meditation. She spaced out each phrase with deliberate attention to each part of the body, "Feel the warmth of the sun on your forehead, on your eyes, on your ears, on your cheeks, on your nose, on your chin, and on your neck. Try to bring full awareness to your face and relax your jaw."

After thirty seconds, Siv said, "Okay, now push back into child's pose, and rest your body. Once there, gently roll your head in circles loosening your neck muscles and balancing your energy. Remember, yoga is about balance and energy. Internal and external, light and dark all have a place in our lives."

Siv continued, "Okay, gently come to a stop, hold still and breathe in deeply for a count of three. Follow my count . . . one . . . two . . . three . . . and hold."

Siv led her yoga army and set an example with several exaggerated inhales and exhales while she counted out loud.

"For our second flow through the sun salutation, I want you to use your imaginations. Let's make our way to the top of the mat again. Feet firmly planted. Sweep your arms up to the sky. Square up to the sun and reach your arms up and grab a star in each hand. There are millions of stars; find the perfect stars for you. Pull yourself up on your toes for a second, and gently come back down. Let's do that same motion two more times. Up for a second, hold, and back down. Up for number three and back down."

The class followed her instructions perfectly, and Siv could see they were enjoying this bit of imagination at work.

"Excellent. Great job everyone!" said Siv excitedly. "You can mirror me in a few more poses. Just flow through the poses at your own pace and when you are ready, we'll meet back standing at the top of our mats when everyone is ready."

Siv's army followed along with a few grunts and groans but mostly they appreciated her gentle guidance on their first-day yoga tour.

"To close today, we'll focus on stretching our quads and shoulders as we reach to our toes. Some of you won't reach all the way down. That's fine. Go only as far as you comfortably can. Alright everyone, use your imaginations again. Balance yourself with your feet about two fists width apart and bend over. Reach right down through the hull of the ship and down into the sand to find some buried treasure. Go slowly. Now squiggle your hands in the sand and move your shoulders like a crab does when it settles into the sand. As you reach down, touch your knees, or your shins, or your ankles or your toes, whatever you can. Remember to listen to your body. Stretch a little bit more than comfortable, but not too much."

Sounds of relaxation could be heard around the deck.

Siv continued, "Alright everyone, find your mats and gently lie down on your backs. Pull your knees in and hold them. Rotate to the left for a few seconds. Now, rotate the other way. Great job, everyone. Bring your hands to the heart-center. We thank our bodies, hearts, and souls for the journey we are on together. Slowly move your hands to your third-eye center at your forehead."

The group followed Siv's every move. Even the most reluctant were now totally engrossed in Siv's directions.

"Each of you feel the light within you. May peace capture your spirit, your heart, and your soul, as together we say, Namaste!"

The group softly murmured, "Namaste."

The Fortune Teller

With a week of daily classes ahead, Siv had helped bond the group. She was pleased with herself. Siv's yoga classes needed good attendance. She was keenly aware that every one of the crew on board was replaceable. She loved to travel and her "perfect" cruise job on the "Joys of Love" answered to the gypsy in her despite the hardship of missing her family. It was a trade-off. We all make those.

She hadn't quite made a full peace with all the travel—at least not yet. One day she felt she was on course; the next, she felt she was screwing up her life. On those days she could feel her mother's anger from across the ocean. She missed her father, too. Her girl-friends at home didn't "get her," and didn't understand her desire to travel. *How could she ever start a family with her nomadic lifestyle?*

On each cruise, Siv noticed the new faces; cooks gone, new bartenders, trainee officers, and excursion personnel changed all the time. She was thankful for the crew who knew the game well enough to become fixtures on each cruise—Raoul, Marietta, even the pool boys. *Did they like leaving their families behind? Maybe they were born to be nomads, too,* Siv thought. Prior to each new cruise, she reached into her soul, questioning herself.

She wasn't sure if she had the crew's mettle, but she hoped so. The Captain's regimen allowed no space for second-guessing. He made it very clear in an unspoken way. He didn't have to say a word. If you got homesick, you were on your own. She saw one guy get deported in Italy. He had complained about being seasick to the ship's steward. That was the kiss of death for him. One minute he was serving tables, the next he was hustled away like leftover garbage on weekly rubbish day.

When Siv got sick two years earlier on a cruise to the Bahamas, she kept it to herself and stayed in her cabin for "feminine reasons." She was mindful not to overuse that excuse lest she be labeled as a "monthly problem"—that was ship talk that essentially discriminated against women. You had to get used to it. The "Joys of Love" was no place for the weak-minded.

After Siv's yoga class, Tina was excited to check out the gym on the way down to lunch. She peered in through the frosted glass door. She pulled the door but there was more resistance than she expected. Undeterred, she planted her left foot firmly and tugged the door open. Tina didn't mind the extra work to enter the gym. She reasoned that the ship doors needed to be secured more tightly than regular doors in the event there were rough seas. She took a quick look in for a "sniff" test—she actually did smell the gym. It was one of the ways she confirmed the gym was clean, safe, and well-maintained. The wall mirrors made the room seem bigger than it was. It was probably only fifteen feet by twenty feet, but everything looked in order. The equipment seemed in good shape. A couple of muscular guys were on the bench machines competing. She didn't care. She didn't give them a second look.

What she did care about was a brochure that caught her eye on the corner shelf near the full-length mirror. On the face of the brochure was an ad to see a fortune teller aboard the ship. Tina was giddy with excitement. The muscle guys could have each other. She found something totally different that made her entire body shiver with delight.

She hadn't had her fortune told in two years. She remembered the last telling. The teller, Julia-Francesca, was an older Spanish woman who used crystals and cards to tell Tina that she saw a cruise in Tina's future, as well as two men. The teller predicted that one of the men was a brainy type and the other an athletic man. One of them had long hair.

Tina delighted in herself that she was now at the very spot her fortune teller had predicted. *Could it be true?* She clung to the hope that fortune tellers like Julia-Francesca could see into the future, or even draw from the past.

Tina's friends chided Tina about her belief in fortune-tellers. *What would they think now?* Was Tina simply living out the planted seeds of the fortune teller? She wanted to believe most of what the teller predicted. Tina thought the teller was certainly very convincing with her powerful and mysterious ways with incense, tea leaves, flickering lights, beads in the doorways, and her three cats—a white cat with blue eyes, a black cat with yellow eyes, and a calico cat with white eyes.

Those cats made Tina uncomfortable. She had never seen such mysterious eyes on cats. Even in the dark, smoky room, she couldn't believe how brightly they shone.

Eyes tell you a lot, especially about men, she thought to herself. "If a man couldn't lock eyes with you, he couldn't be trusted. It was that simple," she told her girlfriends, but they didn't believe her.

Tina found the elevator and pushed "Deck 7." The door opened and Tina entered the brightly lit, mirror-filled elevator cab as it traveled smoothly back down below decks. When Tina walked off the elevator, there was a purple crest sign with gold lettering on the wall facing the elevator. "Cabin 713–See Your Future NOW!" An arrow pointed to the right.

Tina flushed with excitement and quickly walked down the plush, dark-blue, carpeted hallway counting the door numbers on the left side 703, 705, 707, 709, 711—until she finally reached 713. Before she could knock, the door opened and a young deck officer exited as she arrived. He clutched his elbow which had transferred some blood onto his white uniform.

He did not look happy. He brushed by Tina recklessly. He gritted his teeth and without so much as a nod to acknowledge her, he forced her to the opposite side of the narrow hallway. Tina thought this was quite strange but before she could turn and check on the man, he was gone.

Later Tina would learn the cause of the man's bloody elbow. Moonlight, Flora May's calico cat, had left her mark. If Moonlight didn't like a person, she'd scratch them. Moonlight didn't like this guy at all. She had hissed as he left the room.

But for now, Tina merely thought the interaction was odd and interesting. Pretty much everyone related to the cruise line was well-mannered, but not the deck officer who nearly plowed her down in the hallway. She didn't know why, but she sensed trouble was brewing.

Before she could dip her shoulders into the doorframe, a voice called out, "Come right in, sweetie."

Creepy, Tina thought. *How did she know I was here?*

"I know you." Flora May said. "You are the woman the men were ga-ga over at the pool yesterday. Can't say I blame them."

Embarrassed, Tina didn't know what to say. "Oh, just men being men, I guess."

"Sit down," Flora May said in a hoarse voice. Tina wondered if she had been crying.

Flora May covered her eyes with an old opera mask as she sat behind a low-hanging brass candelabra. It held three candles that cast a warm glow within the cabin. Flora May had a calico cat with white eyes in her lap. Tina felt a shiver go up her spine.

Immediately, Flora May sensed a spirit in the room. She stood up. The cat jumped on the table. "Moonlight, watch your tail in the flames!" Flora May scolded the cat. The woman didn't appear to be over five feet tall. Her fingers spread wide as if gathering something in the air directly in front of her. The joints on her hands were swollen and pressed through her thin skin. Flora May took a deep breath in and exhaled forcefully.

"He's here. He's in the room with us."

"Who?" asked Tina nervously.

"I can't quite tell yet," said Flora May. "But I feel his presence. He is agitated. He wants to pass through from the other side to give you something. I'm seeing flowers—maybe roses—and a ring. He hasn't been able to break through. The flowers mean something to him. They are pink and yellow."

Flora May sat back in her chair and closed her eyes. Tina leaned in, anxiously awaiting more information about this mystery man.

"He's lost somebody. He needs your help," said Flora May with a pained expression.

Tina was intrigued. This was real. She could feel it.

Moonlight jumped off the table onto a wall sconce, clinging with her claws. The candles flickered and then darkened. There was a cold blast of air and the candles went out. Tina shivered again.

"He's leaving now," said Flora May.

Both women took a deep breath in and exhaled.

The whole thing went by so quickly. One minute Tina was entranced by Flora May and the spirit, and then it was pitch dark in the room. The cat was clinging spider-like to the wall. The room was deadly still. Tina got up shaking and fumbled for her wallet. "I'd . . . I'd like to pay you."

"No," said Flora May. "Your spirit friend is strong. He'll be back. This doesn't happen often, especially with this intensity. Come back tomorrow at about the same time. Wear something red under your clothes and bring a flower."

Tina was confused but knew she would be back.

"One more thing," Flora May said. "Your heart has been broken. The spirits tell me that this must happen to find true love. Love itself must be banished to unthinkable fire so that the heart hardens like King Arthur's stone-penetrating sword. Only then, like a flower in the spring, love rekindles."

Flora May's eyes shut. Tina wondered if Flora May herself had a torn and broken heart.

In that moment Tina saw the fortune-teller's jaw tighten as if she were remembering something very painful. The woman slumped in her chair. There was silence for a few moments and then Flora May's eyes opened and she spoke with intense clarity.

"I see someone . . . older. A man. He's coming toward you."

Suddenly Flora May bolted upright and with a strained voice said, "Fight for that love my dear. You *must*! It will give you great joy. I can see it clearly. You cannot go through life with such a burden."

Flora May stopped. Tears rolled down her cheeks.

Tina slowly and quietly let out a breath she didn't realize she had been holding. She reached for Flora May's hand. Images sliced through her mind too fast for recall. She blinked as Moonlight jumped on the wall to the flickering lights. Flora May's hands curled tightly around Tina's. Tina could feel the pain Flora May's clairvoyance caused the tortured seer.

Tina knew she would come back the next day. She couldn't resist.

Tina was anxious. The cat and Flora May had frazzled her nerves. Tina decided to go outside and grab lunch at one of the high deck bars to see if it might settle her down. She was seated at a private table overlooking the crisp blue waters of the Caribbean. She sat for a while taking in all that had just unfolded with Flora

May. She began questioning everything. *Was it all fake, or did Flora May really have the power to see into Tina's past and future?*

The waiter brought her a menu and she ordered the salmon en croute with fresh grilled asparagus with a white wine butter sauce. It was another pièce de résistance by Georgio and Marietta. As Tina ate by herself overlooking the water, the perfect spices melted in her mouth. She couldn't help thinking about the two guys Julia Francesca had foreseen.

The "Joys of Love" was becoming more interesting than she could have ever imagined. *What would be revealed to her next? Would she get a message from the mysterious spirit?*

Tina was sure something big was in store.

7

Brains vs. Muscles

After a relaxing morning and a delicious lunch, Tina decided to check out the gym. She rarely missed a day of working out and didn't want her time on the "Joys of Love" to interrupt her routine. The gym was impeccably clean and outfitted with all the machines she would need to keep up her routine this week. Each station had a neatly folded towel and a bottle of Evian water.

As she stepped on the treadmill and leaned over to stretch her hamstrings, two very different-looking men came out of nowhere and positioned themselves on the treadmills beside her. One was a very muscle-bound guy and the other looked brainy, like an academic. It wasn't obvious at first if the two men knew each other, but they looked familiar to her. She may have seen them at the pool or walking on board the ship. She couldn't recall for sure. They both ran beside her for her entire run of five miles. She could tell they were both struggling, but neither was willing to give up. *Maybe they're hoping to meet me?* she thought.

As she stepped off the treadmill, they both did too. She could hear both men sigh in relief. Tina had given them a run for their money.

Tina walked over to the stretching area and they followed behind like lost puppies. The brainy looking one wore black, large-rimmed glasses that covered his nose.

"Hi there, I'm Justin, from Chicago,"

With a quick elbow in Justin's ribs, the other man stepped in front of Justin and introduced himself. "Hi, I'm Fabian, from New York. And you are?"

Stepping back in with a shove, Justin blurted out, "She is probably bothered by rude people. I'm so happy to meet you, Ms.?" as he held out his hand. The two friends seemed harmless enough despite themselves.

"I'm Tina. Nice to meet you both. I'm from the South," she shared, over-emphasizing a sweet, Southern drawl, but unwilling to give up more information at this juncture.

"A southern belle," said the nerdy one with interest.

Fabian quickly chirped, "I stayed in New Orleans for a couple of years; sweetest place on earth." He hoped he got it right.

"Actually," the nerdy Justin retorted, "the sweetest spot on earth is right here in front of Ms. Tina, wouldn't you say, Ms. Tina?"

Flattered and annoyed at the same time, Tina responded, "Well boys, this has been stimulating enough, but I'd like to finish stretching alone, if you don't mind. You guys have been interesting, and I'm sure I'll see more of you on one of the excursions. Bye, fellas!"

She stepped away. Tina wanted to get some fresh air and alone time out on the deck after stretching. She didn't leave them a hint of where she was going.

Justin's single story started with a long line of women to whom he could never commit. He didn't know why. Maybe it was in his DNA. Whenever he got too close to a woman, he'd find something wrong with them. *She's too pushy*, he'd think to himself, or *She's too tight with money and always yacking with her girlfriends*. Or he would pull himself away by burying himself in work or some other activity.

When he thought about his inability to commit, he often thought of his first serious relationship. It was with a cute girl named Maddie from upstate New York. She had a crush on him. They'd talk on the phone for hours. She loved animals and worked in an animal shelter.

One day after attending a wedding together, she started nudging the conversation toward his future plans. She wanted to bring their relationship to the next level. He wasn't ready. He wondered what would have happened to their relationship if he was less judgmental and more into the place she was at.

Justin had a few married friends. One had two small children. The kids were delightful, but his buddy had changed from a happy-go-lucky friend who went out almost every Friday night with his group to a rock-solid "No" on fun nights with the guys. Justin couldn't see himself traveling down that path and could feel the separation between himself and Maddie grow—Friday night by Friday night.

Maddie, on the other hand, took great pains to share her joy on how happy their married friends seemed to be. It didn't take long for Justin to distance himself from Maddie after that wedding.

He came to dislike weddings for a million other reasons: the cost, the pettiness, and the boredom of the ceremonies. He just didn't appreciate the whole "thing," whether it was the bridesmaids' matching dresses, the formality, the alcohol silliness that took place, or the faux importance of it all. In just ten years, he had seen more than a few of his friends' perfect weddings end in divorces. It made him question whether marriage made sense.

For her part, Maddie quickly became an unhappy camper when Justin didn't return her phone calls within a few hours. They never made love. As time went on, Maddie was so mad that she started spreading rumors among his friends that he might be gay.

That made things go from bad to ugly to irreversibly bad. It was a shame because he liked Maddie. He just wasn't ready. He wasn't a loner, but he couldn't see himself all "familied up" at such an early point in his life. Justin delayed contacting her until Maddie eventually just fell off his preferred call queue on his cell phone.

That less-than-perfect ending started Justin on a trail of "end-ships" instead of long-lasting friendships.

Fabian had a similar story. He was a handsome guy from a large Italian family. His siblings were always hooking him up. And he was always failing them. He had had so many bad dates that he wanted to enter a contest and be crowned, "The good, bad-date guy" to confirm his suspicions about his improbable un-likeability. It didn't make sense. He was handsome and witty and he didn't feel he was hard to get along with. Yet he stood on the sideline and watched a parade of his friends tie the knot. He just never got a powerful enough urge to cross that bridge.

So here he was fighting with his friend Justin on a singles cruise to catch what? He didn't know.

Tina was pretty enough. But he'd had plenty of chances with pretty women. He wondered if he'd ever find a mate—someone who'd appreciate him for who he was, not what he looked like, or what he could do for them. He was embarrassed to admit to himself that he hadn't met a woman in a long time that was "deeper than a puddle," to use his uncle Joe's favorite saying. Thinking those thoughts made him laugh. Fabian was no Einstein, and he knew it.

For a dozen years, his job as a city inspector kept him busy, and with his family looking out for him, there was always a cute date available. But now that he was in his thirties, it seemed that a window was closing. He didn't know there were women on board the ship who felt the exact same way as he did. "The girl" for him had to have depth and a sense of humor. He wondered if his true mate existed. And if so, *where was she? How could he find someone that was right for him? Would this singles cruise provide the answers?*

Connecting people was Sheila's job on the "Joys of Love." She would try and throw Fabian and Justin lifelines at the masquerade party later in the evening. Sheila had her wings spread around two nice single women on the cruise from the northeastern United States. Katrina and her friend Jillian were both professional women who worked at MIT in Boston and were vacationing together. Both were looking for eligible guys who were a *lot* deeper than a puddle, but not so full of themselves as their workmates were back home. Sheila had encouraged the women to come to the party and expect to meet some better-than-average men. Her fingers were crossed for these four.

Next to the dress up formal, the masquerade party was Sheila's favorite event. On party night, Sheila sized up each of the guests and brought them into the costume room she had commandeered from maintenance. The room was filled with top hats, masks, gypsy dresses, parasols, costume jewelry, and other easy-to-wear, character-assuming paraphernalia. To complete the transformations, Sheila had a make-up artist that each guest would see before the party. Larger than life eyebrows, whiskers, and handlebar mustaches were standard fare.

With her encouragement, on party night, guests would enter that room as self-doubters and exit minutes later as confident and dazzling movie actresses or swash-buckling pirates ready to meet their counterparts and conquer distant worlds arm in arm. Sheila hoped that the fun world she created would help unlock the hidden and likeable personalities of her guests.

When Tina left the gym, she ran into Sheila. "Our first masquerade party is tonight. I so hope you'll join us," Sheila gushed with excitement.

"You bet, can't wait," replied Tina. Tina thoughts drifted immediately to what she might wear for the masquerade party. She was eager to see the costumes Sheila had available. As a child and through her teens, Tina loved dress-up dates and small parties with her family and friends. In her childhood dreams, Tina was a fairy who could magically make things happen with the touch of a wand. To this day she had kept those wistful ideas alive. *Could she bloom at the right time for once, at the masquerade party?*

With both spirited and uneasy thoughts coursing through her mind, Tina decided to get some fresh air on the forward deck facing the sun. Before Tina settled into a chaise lounge, she pushed two nearby chairs several feet away. She wanted to send a message. She had a wide-open view of the horizon; exactly what the doctor ordered. That prescription did not include anyone within earshot of her special private paradise view.

Billowy, powder-puff cumulus clouds created island and peninsula shapes against the pastel blue sky. There could be nothing better on the second day at sea than drenching herself in sunshine *alone*.

Alone wasn't in the cards.

"Hey dumb-ass," a gruff bearded guy with a bandana, cursed at her. "Didn't you see my coffee? You are in my chair."

At first Tina jumped up ready to punch the guy, but then she looked more closely. There was something wrong. He had one eye. His right eye rolled up in his sun-burned face no matter which way he turned his head. She had an uncle named Paulie with one eye, but his was stuck in one place.

Tina looked him in the eye and gave a pathetic, "Sorry."

No question why this guy was single. She immediately felt bad for even thinking that.

Close Encounter

On this particular afternoon, Tina wore a pastel blue, string bikini. By chance, it matched the sky perfectly. She had brought a different bathing suit for every day of the six-day cruise. Some of the tops covered her breasts all the way out to the sides of her "B" cups. The other tops she brought cut in different ways over her cleavage. She was careful not to wear the same cut each day so that she could get a nice, uniform tan.

She learned this from experience. When she was younger, Tina got quite a burn when she fell asleep at the beach one summer day. From then on, she set her alarm for an hour any time she was in the sun. She set her alarm for 4:00 p.m. It was time to relax and do some reading.

She had packed a couple of People magazines, her yoga work-out guides, and a couple of Seek-a-Word puzzle books. She delighted in filling out the word puzzles quickly. It sharpened her vocabulary and pattern recognition. She reminded herself how much she wanted to meet a smart man—no dummies for her. Maybe a scientist or a journalist, a business owner, or a doctor, although she had met a few medical types who were too much into their careers to be relationship material.

As she picked up her Seek-a-Word book, she reached on top of her head for her glasses. *Uhhh*, she thought. *I forgot my damn sunglasses. I must go back to my cabin and get them.*

As she got up, from the corner of her eye she saw an older man in a tan fedora and a Hawaiian tourist shirt with red and green tulips on it. He had tripped and was stumbling toward her. *Does anyone really think those shirts are stylish?* she asked herself.

She groaned silently. She wouldn't be caught dead in one of those gross shirts. She felt strongly about what she and her girlfriends back home called "the stupid look." They would always giggle and tell each other when they spotted those shirts. It was a secret and silly ritual that played out when they got together, like looking for a car with one headlight when they were kids.

Unfortunately, before she could adjust her path away from the shirt and the guy in it, she had projected herself in the wardrobe-mistakes direction. She couldn't avoid him. As he tripped, he inadvertently lunged forward toward her. She caught him like a wide receiver catches a football on a quick return route. He fell into her and brushed his face into her chest.

His grey beard scuffed over her chest leaving a red mark at the low point of her cleavage. She bristled but tried to calm herself.

"I'm so sorry," said the red-faced man with a full-mouth grimace. As they righted themselves, she pulled back and took a better look. He was an older gentleman in excellent shape with large shoulders.

"I don't know what happened. I'm completely embarrassed, Miss," he said as he pulled himself away from her. "I'm hoping the ship listed a bit, and it wasn't just me being completely uncoordinated? I think my clogs caught on the edge of the deck."

Really? Tina thought to herself. She looked down in the direction he came from trying to see any "edge." She'd be telling her girlfriends about this one for sure.

The Hawaiian shirt guy couldn't help but notice her perfume. The sweetness of her scent together with her perspiration was on his nose. The smell—a faint scent of roses and cashmere—was fantastic. It excited him. Still clutching her forearm to brace himself, he asked, "What is that beautiful perfume you are wearing?"

Tina pulled her arm back and stammered, "I think it is Victoria Secret's Elegance."

"Do they have that in the commissary? I'd love to buy it for you for the trouble I caused."

The older gentleman had a bold way about him, even though his meet-up style left a lot to be desired. *What the heck*, she thought, and then said, "Why that would be nice."

For a second, he fancied himself with a chance at getting lucky with the beautiful women he had unintentionally accosted. To make amends, he hoped, he quickly and eagerly assured her, "I'll bring it to the next Yoga class."

"Ok," said Tina half-heartedly. Immediately she second-guessed herself. *Is this a mistake? Should I have politely declined? Oh yes. It was a mistake,* she thought. She quickly pulled back, and said, "That's okay. Please don't." She was trying not to make a scene, but in fact, that is exactly what they had done. Instantly, she disliked herself for her quick rush to judgment and dismissive tone. She knew she was better than that.

"Look," she said, "That's very nice of you. Please don't worry about it. I've stumbled a couple of times myself on board the ship. There's really no need to make amends for anything. You have a nice day."

She smiled and started toward her cabin feeling better about herself. The stumble and trip, stupid-look guy was impressed. He made a mental note to get the perfume first thing in the morning.

Before she walked away, stumble-and-trip guy asked, "What's your name?"

"I'm Tina." she replied.

"Pleased to meet you Tina, and I'm really sorry. I'm Enrique."

They shook hands and acknowledged each other with another smile before heading off in their separate directions.

Enrique took a minute to right himself after his embarrassing episode with Tina and headed off to check out the cruise itinerary and to see Sheila. He had lots of questions about the amenities and activities aboard the ship.

"Sheila, how are you? I'm Enrique. I messaged you earlier." Sheila wore a short-sleeved button down top with the Red Heart insignia of her "Joys of Love" uniform on her left sleeve. On her right sleeve, she had a cute cupid pin with an archer's arrow pointing at the heart on her other sleeve. Sheila's grandmother had made the pin and given it to her for her sixteenth birthday. It was her treasure. She always traveled with it. It reminded her of her grandmother's love for her grandpa. They were together for thirty years when grandpa passed.

Her grandmother stoically carried on passing her love to Sheila and her family. She was one tough cookie. Sheila was glad to have those genes.

Sheila always thought that the man for her would notice the heart and ask about the cupid pin. In five years of cruising, only women asked about it. When it came to jewelry, women were much more observant. Apparently her special guy hadn't gotten the memo.

Enrique asked, "Tell me about your masquerade party. Is it hard to get people to come?"

"Why, not at all," said Sheila. "Especially the women. We all love to dress up."

"What about the men?" continued Enrique.

"Well, as you know, it's a singles cruise, and the men kind of follow. I just have to give them a nudge in the right direction and let them know how much women enjoy the party."

Sheila took the opportunity to lasso Enrique. "You'll be joining us, won't you?" She gauged Enrique to be super smart and pitched him, "There are lots of smart women looking for handsome men like you!"

Nicely done, thought Enrique. "Yes, I'll be coming. What shall I wear?"

Sheila said, "Meet me this evening at 1800, and I'll show you our costumes." Sheila's intuition kicked in, and correctly guessed that he knew the maritime clock.

"1800 hours, great. Where should I meet you?" asked Enrique.

"On the third deck, outside of maintenance. The door is marked by two older, blue and yellow ocean buoys on either side of the door, and it has a black pirate's skull and crossbones on the door. You can't miss it."

"Good, I'll see you there," said Enrique. He was pleased to see Sheila's take-charge persona. He loved to see punctual, well-run activities wherever he traveled. He wondered whether Tina would be attending and decided to query Sheila.

He wasn't sure how to express his interest without coming across too eagerly.

"Sheila, there were a couple of ladies at the pool. I was wondering..." Sheila saved him and interrupted, "Oh, yes, I told the ladies at the pool that the party was mandatory for them."

Sheila winked at Enrique.

"Tina will be at the party."

9

Masquerade Party

The party started at 7:30 p.m. just as the sun was setting. Sheila had arranged hanging multi-colored lights to rim the dance floor. It was a perfect evening for dance and dress-up. Excitement filled the air. The ship rolled slightly in the sea from an ocean storm several hundred miles from their location. A light breeze at the bar gently buffeted the guests.

The staff dressed in Hawaiian costumes and passed out complimentary pineapple and rum drinks with little turquoise umbrellas popping over the sugared rims of the glasses.

Per Sheila's plan, the guests weren't easy to identify in their costumes. She hoped it would make it easier for them to make new friends.

Off the stern in the distance the sun held onto a bronze halo as it began to dip into the water on the horizon. The sun stared back at the ship through the water as it lit up schools of minnows and other small ocean fish jumping at the surface of the water. Seagulls dove down into the water and reappeared with their necks straining as they gulped the unlucky first course of their dinner.

Over twenty waiters and waitresses descended on the deck with the "Joys of Love's" first course. Each of the server's trays featured exotic assortments of shellfish displayed perfectly. There were juicy shrimp, garlicy mussels, King crabcakes and clam shells nestled in lettuce and other greens. Bright yellow sweet corn halves surrounded lobsters and made the red shells glow in contrast.

The trays were custom-made iron that could withstand the Sterno chafing fuel used to keep the charcoal and butter-crusted lobster appetizers warm.

As the waiters uncovered their polished chrome surprises, "oohs" and "ahhs" were heard all around the ballroom in anticipation of their next gastronomic delight. Georgio and Marietta had outdone themselves yet again. Guests applauded as the waiters spun the culinary art down on to their tables.

Glasses clanged in the background amidst the murmuring appreciations of the guests. Bartenders shook their drink concoctions in stainless containers before pouring them into chilled martini glasses with green olives pierced by small green plastic swords.

Raoul worked the corner station and yelled, "Tamarra, order up! Janiece table seven! Donna, get me more glasses!" Ice could be heard sloshing into the mixed drink orders Raoul raced to fill. An occasional loud toast came from a happy contingent of Polish guests at a table in the corner. "Nastrovia" (to your health) echoed loudly into the air.

Between the Sterno flames and the loud chirps of, "It's lobster," the entire seating area came alive. The beautiful serving trays mirrored a kaleidoscope of colors off the guests' eyes as the flames danced brightly. Half oranges and limes were nestled amongst the freshest seafood in the world. How could the seafood not be fresh? Divers worked the seabed whenever the ship was at anchor. Beds of vibrant-colored arugula and micro-greens accompanied each tray. The buttery smell of beurre blanc sauce filled the air as puddles of it glistened on the silver trays.

The ballroom was a feast for the senses. Sheila looked around and felt very pleased with how the evening was unfolding.

She had arranged for a cover band to play country music and oldies. Several of the men stood around a table laughing and joking while they took stock of each other's costumes.

In the spirit of fun, Ricky, the young engineer from Ecuador, styled himself like the famed Spanish conquistador and swordsman Zorro. Sheila fitted him with a mask, mustache, bandana, cape, plastic sword, and a fake ponytail. He had a bit of trouble with the ponytail and asked for help. "Hey Sheila," he asked, "Can you tighten this ponytail? I move a lot on the dance floor and want to be sure it stays in place. I've got to keep my machismo image."

Sheila came to him and asked him to turn for her so that she could adjust the hair clasp on the ponytail. She fixed the ponytail and exclaimed, "Perfecto." In his dancing mode, Ricky pirouetted quickly showing his well-practiced dance moves. When he stopped, Sheila and Ricky were face to face—nostrils flared and separated by no more than a cat's whisker. Sheila could smell his body and his musk cologne.

She took a deep breath. She hadn't been that close to a man in a year or more. Her thoughts wandered as she unconsciously moistened her lower lip. She didn't realize her subtle movement or its effect on Ricky. He noticed and smiled to himself. It was a hope-filled moment.

Sheila's mind drifted as she visualized Ricky spinning her around the dance floor; a magical moment for Zorro, the matador, and his beautiful senorita. In her mind, their feet didn't touch the floor as he spun her around. Their combined spirits floated them on notes of music above the floor. She thought to herself, *He is smashing in that outfit!*

"Hey Sheila," Fabian interjected loudly to get her attention. Without knowing it, Fabian dashed Sheila's private dream. She exhaled for a minute and to gather herself back for her guests as Fabian continued, "I was wondering about the face painting."

Fabian was outfitted as a wrestling champion. He wore a six-inch thick belt with a medallion at the center. Fabian was proud of his gym-crafted body. Muscles rippled from his chest down through his ripped muscle stack. He caught a glimpse of himself in the mirror. It made him feel it was worth all the long workouts. He needed some eye-black and perhaps some red lightning strikes on his cheeks.

Fabian opted for a bandana as his only extra garment. There wasn't much left to the imagination. Fabian hoped the ladies at the party would appreciate his arm rocks and tight abs.

With a giggle, Sheila yelled back, "Handlebar mustaches. Ladies love those. You'll sweep them off their feet."

As she pulled away from Fabian, she recognized how much daydreaming about Ricky had impacted her, and her responses to Fabian. She had to watch herself. She had, after all, just been lifted off her feet in her daydream dance with Ricky. She wondered if Ricky felt it too. Ricky was younger, enough to give her pause. She had never thought of herself as a "cougar" before this fleeting attraction with Ricky. She hoped no one had noticed their brief moment. But one set of eyes caught the lightning that flashed between them.

Who? Sheila would learn later which of the guests had prying eyes. But for now the game was on. Music filled the air.

The costumed guests were difficult to identify. It added to the intrigue. Fabian saw an attractive taller woman in a Cinderella guise. He approached, bowed, and asked for the dance.

She, equally attracted, curtsied and extended her hand. They were off. As she followed his lead, she thought to herself, *Yes, that's what I needed. A handsome man with a great physique. What is he really like? No matter. Tonight is for fun.*

The two of them marched to the center flaunting their costumes, hard bodies, and assumed identities. They looked to be having a great time.

Sheila looked on with pride. These were the events she lived for. She knew she was earning her keep and it truly pleased her.

She looked over the crowd hoping to see Tina and maybe Enrique. What were they up to?

10

A Peculiar Start to a Romance

Whoever owned the prying eyes, one thing for certain is that it wasn't Justin and Jillian. They were too busy building their courage while they sorted out their own dating discomforts. Silly as it sounds, they were afraid to meet anyone. Yet, with Sheila's persistent urging, they convinced themselves to participate.

Jillian wore a pink princess outfit with a swooping neckline, and a tall, bright red hat adorned with a yellow satin bow. Sheila's master masquerade costume for Jillian included a giant cubic zirconia necklace that shined over Jillian's ample bosom.

Justin saw her from across the dance floor and was smitten. He was also nervous—too nervous to go after her. His stomach was a mess. It started to churn at the thought of introducing himself. He tried to talk himself out of being nervous, knowing that everyone feels this way—guys and girls; even though none of the girls he had dated openly admitted it. It was a closely held gender secret—akin to a national security secret—to be guarded with one's life.

Sheila, who was always on the look-out for possible hook-ups for her guests, took notice of their reluctance to approach each other. Justin and Jillian were about fifteen feet apart when Sheila swooped over, grabbed Justin by the hand and led him to Jillian.

"Jillian, have you met my friend, Justin?" she asked.

"Well, he's one of our very special guests and a pirate too. Why don't you two chat and I'll come back and check in on you in a few minutes."

Sheila whispered in Jillian's ear as she brushed by, "Justin is really charming but shy. Kind of like you."

As Sheila walked away, Justin's stomach was in a frenzy. He decided he had to be honest with Jillian.

"I am so sorry but you are so pretty and I feel like a twelve-year-old boy in junior high school. My stomach and nerves are going crazy," Justin admitted shyly.

"I feel the same way," Jillian responded with a girlish giggle.

Justin looked down at her cautiously, like one looks at a toad refusing to move on a pathway they are trying to traverse.

"For real?" he said.

Jillian tried to answer but could only muster another laugh in response. It wasn't a tiny, girlish, you-could-barely-hear-it laugh. It wasn't prim and proper at all. It was the kind of laugh that comes out through your nose; a snort. It escaped. Damn. Everyone has a friend that does that. Jillian was that friend.

Her laugh tickled Justin's funny bone in just the right way. He started loudly snorting in response. The more he looked at her, the more he couldn't control his own laughter.

In an instant, they were busy beginning their potential relationship, laughing in joint embarrassment of their own and each other's laughs. They were having too much fun with each other to be nervous.

Their laughter was as spontaneous and contagious as the music-to-the-ears laughter one hears when a child uncontrollably laughs from a parent's squeamish tickles with their noses into their little bellies as they goad them on to louder and louder screams of delight. It seems to happen on plane rides often.

Justin and Jillian were now having nose-running laughs. People noticed and couldn't help but stare. Then those people started laughing. The stares were "good fun stares" if such a thing exists.

Justin's and Jillian's nervousness vanished among the silliness. They both were so relieved. Out of the corner of her eye, Jillian saw Sheila coming.

She said, "Justin, stop laughing" with a begging look in her eyes.

He didn't.

With even more urgency Jillian pleaded "Stop, Justin! Stop!"

He couldn't. The whole scene poured gas on the fire.

She begged him, but only between snorts.

"I'm going to pee myself if you don't stop."

"Really," Justin said with a fake, sad puppy look. "So sorry for your discomfort."

The door keeping Justin's mischievous imp locked away swung wide open. He couldn't resist. He started making faces. The kind you do with your friends or siblings to goof around. He twisted his jaw to the right, pushed his tongue out to the left, and broke into more laughter.

Sheila stopped back in to see them with a cheery, "So what's happening with you two?"

They just looked at each other and laughed harder and harder.

Sheila had an incredulous, questioning look. "Really now, what *is* happening with you two?"

Jillian was holding her legs locked together. Her stomach was tight, as was her bladder. She reached out and shoved Justin adding an imploring stop-please look.

Sheila's repeat of the question didn't help either one of them answer. Not one bit. The whole scene was too funny to absorb. Jillian had always been too tense on dates. Justin's honesty was the perfect antidote to Jillian's irrational insecurity, and it unlocked her personality.

They had contagious laughter; all three of them. Sheila started laughing even though she didn't know what the three of them were laughing about, which made Justin and Jillian laugh even harder than before.

In fact, neither of them had ever laughed so hard in their lives.

Sheila stepped back and said, "Oh my. Whatever you guys are on, I want everyone to get it."

"Oh no you don't." said Jillian.

That caused Justin and Jillian to fall into each other's arms laughing uncontrollably, but not for long. Jillian had to rush off to the ladies room.

Sheila had seen a lot of first dates, but this one was truly an outlier. She couldn't figure out what had happened.

Before Sheila could get an explanation, Tina came into view with a question about Enrique, the older gentleman who seemed suspiciously secretive. Sheila would have to circle back to Justin and Jillian later.

Sheila thought to herself, *What was Enrique up to anyway?*

She was about to find out.

11

Older Men and Money

Tina had only dated one older man. Jake was a 36-year-old guy back in South Carolina where she went to college. She was 26 at the time—a ten-year difference. She met him through her friend Marie.

Tina and Marie travelled with three other friends, Susan, Molly, and Jennifer, to see their favorite college team play a football game at a nearby college. On the way home, they got a flat tire. The girls called everyone they knew for help until finally Marie reached her dad who convinced her older brother Jake to fix the tire. Jake had to drive about sixty miles to meet them.

Jake was about six feet tall with red hair and an athletic build. He worked at a garage while in high school and easily knew how to make the repair. Jake arrived at the convenience store where they made their rescue call in an old, red Chevy Impala convertible he had restored. He wore faded blue jeans and a brown, muscle T-shirt. The girls were around the back of the car looking in the trunk at the spare tire when he arrived.

None of them had learned how to change a flat tire. They hadn't even taken the jack out let alone the spare tire.

Jake walked to back of the car and said, "You ladies seem to have this pretty much under control, huh?"

Jake was playfully embarrassing the girls and his sister, and he knew it. It didn't take long before Marie had enough of her older brother's antics and demanded, "Jake, are you going to fix it or what?"

Jake responded, "Now, Missy Marie, I traveled a good distance to get here, and I'm going to enjoy the mess you got yourselves into. Three years ago I tried to show you how to fix a flat tire, and you were too damn busy. Remember?" He enjoyed rubbing it in.

Tina understood Jake's playful and partly punitive tone as he made his little sister squirm. Marie was the most boisterous of her friends, and Tina had always thought Marie's ego could use a little adjustment.

Jake continued, "You know, Dad tried to show you too. But you were so smart and had to get off to college. You make sure to tell him I fixed the tire, okay?"

"You haven't fixed it yet," chirped Marie.

Tina looked at her three friends and said, "Marie, why didn't you tell us your brother was a hunk?" The girls giggled. Marie smirked in disgust.

Jake looked at Tina and said, "You seem to be the smart one. Why don't you give me a hand here? Grab the jack and the tire iron. I'll get the spare."

Tina liked the attention he gave her and began flirting with Jake. She bent over the trunk pretending to look in the far corner and said, "Jake, I can't find the tire iron. Can you see if you can find it?"

Joyce and the others huddled away from the car and watched Tina bend over the trunk. Sally watched Tina and said to the others, "Are you kidding me. That little tramp."

Despite her jealous friends' attempt to derail her, Tina managed to build a rapport with Jake. One thing led to another, and soon they were dating. Jake had an apartment and Tina would stay over occasionally. At first things went smoothly, but over time their age difference started to cause problems.

One night Jake asked Tina to go to a concert with an oldie's revival band. Tina looked at him like she had swallowed a toad and said, "You and the septuagenarians will have to make that dance without me."

Jake was insulted. That was a strong culture slap Tina had thrown at him. Yet the biggest difference between the two of them wasn't culture. It was technology. There is a difference between a guy who understands what an "app" is and a guy who can't make a simple restaurant reservation online. The older people she knew were dinosaurs with technology.

Those same thoughts surfaced when she thought of Enrique, her new Hawaiian shirt friend. If he was anything like Jake, she'd put all her thoughts about him on probation, or in the trash bin.

At yoga the next day, Enrique arrived with her favorite perfume as promised, and a small bouquet of roses from the flower shop.

Nice, she thought to herself. It was also nice that he didn't make it overly obvious in front of the others. One day was enough for the two of them to be the center of attention. When he arrived,

Enrique motioned Tina to the side and pulled out the gifts, a kind of classy little move. It softened her up a bit toward him.

Turned out he was a software designer and an investor. She thought to herself, okay, he'll easily pass the technology test. She still wasn't sure if Enrique knew her name. He definitely did.

"Tina, I really can't tell you how badly I felt after falling into you."

"Don't worry. It's okay," she assured him.

Enrique continued, "If there is anything I can do for you, just let me know."

"Nah. Let's just enjoy the class," she responded as she turned her attention back to yoga.

Enrique wore a nice, lightweight, beige linen-colored top. *Nice choice*, she thought to herself. *He ditched the obnoxious shirt. I'll keep the door for him open for a little while.*

Tina's grandmother's voice echoed in her head. "Now sweetie, never mind marrying for love. We all get divorced anyway. You find yourself a nice old guy close to the deep-six, and bring him on home to Granny. I'll tell you if he's good enough for you."

Tina smiled to herself. She was named after Granny Theresa. As Tina remembered that day, she shook her head absentmindedly and took in a deep breath and pushed out a great big smile. Her Granny was a firecracker.

Enrique looked in Tina's direction. He loved to see that smile. He hoped it was for him.

"Is that your spot?" he asked.

Tina jolted out of her "granny-trance" and said, "Yes. I like the front."

Tina set her mat near Siv. Enrique went to the opposite side of the floor. She watched as he stripped off his outer shorts revealing skin-tight, thigh-high yoga shorts underneath. His large quads imprinted through the fine blue fabric nicely. *He is an athlete. Hmm? It's getting interesting,* Tina thought.

Tina slipped out of her joggers exposing her black, thin, nylon yoga pants. As she bent over to pick up her newly discarded joggers, she glimpsed backwards under her arms in Enrique's direction and noticed that he was checking her out too.

Siv motioned everyone with a slight bow and hands together in thanks. She began her normal routine.

"We'll start today with our breathing and some easy peasy relaxing. I see some of you are back for a second tour. Welcome back. And for you newcomers, fit right in and enjoy. Any questions?"

Her soft and firm voice invited everyone to settle in and relax.

Siv was in heaven. Tina was in heaven too, on a cruise ship and thinking she was exactly where she was supposed to be. That didn't happen very often in her life. Tina enjoyed Siv's class. Tina practiced yoga consistently and it showed. She also had worked hard to afford this cruise and reserve the time too. Knowing how fleeting moments like this were, Tina was hell-bent on making the best of it. She closed her eyes, taking it all in, and saturated herself in the open air.

After about twenty minutes, Siv brought the class to completion with her standard Shavasana routine, followed by, "Bring your hands to your third-eye center, and together we say 'Namaste.' Thank you!"

In a blink, as if it hadn't happened at all, the class ended. Tina was disappointed how quickly the time had gone by. She was amazed at how many things in life disappeared in exactly that way.

Tina's mind had wandered again. Yet, Tina felt refreshed by the salt air, the sunlight, the Caribbean breeze, the karma of the group and the release of her inner tensions.

Tina was very happy as she gathered her gear and put her mat back in the bin. She smiled and waved at Enrique as she excitedly headed off to see Flora May for another reading. Enrique had hoped to chat but had his own itinerary to follow. He had to meet the Captain to see the new navigation system.

What to Wear to Meet Her Spirit Friend?

On the third day of the cruise, at about 3:00 p.m., Tina sat in her room looking through her clothes. Flora May had told her to wear something red under her clothes. Tina thought about the cute red panties from Victoria's Secret. *Too much. Maybe the red pendant.*

Then she remembered the red bathing suit she had packed. She found it on an impromptu shopping day. It was a rainy, throwaway day on her weekend visit to see a friend in Atlantic City, New Jersey. Tina walked into a boutique on the famous Boardwalk looking for the elusive bathing suit that fit both her bottom and her top.

After plying through fifty or more suits, she found a red, flowered, B-top suit that she loved, and went to the counter. "Do you have the bottoms of this suit in a medium?" she asked. She followed the clerk to another section of the store where together they flipped another hundred or so hangers back and forth. She swore she had tried on 150 suits before she found that one.

She thought to herself, *Guys just don't realize the torture buying a bathing suit represents for women.* Most suits either fit her top, and not her bottom, or vice-versa. The bottom cuts often made her belly look too big, or her cheeks were overly exposed. Thong suits—even worse. She was jealous of girls who could pull those off. Her, not so much.

She settled on the red bathing suit with its bold yellow, red, and green flower pattern.

She couldn't decide on her cover up. She had brought a nice sheer wrap but wanted more cover than that could provide. She settled instead for her daisy duke shorts with their neatly combed fringes at the bottom of the legs. There was plenty of "juice" in those shorts.

Before heading to Flora May's, Tina decided to go up to her favorite lounging place on the high deck. She grabbed a couple of spiral notebooks to write some more on themes for the articles she envisioned. She knew her writing had to engage and entice, and hoped her time on the upper deck would provide inspiration.

She knew young singles did less reading and watched more videos. She thought to herself, *If I want to draw them away from movies, TikTok, Instagram, and YouTube, I have to grab their attention with sex, love, and adventure.* She wondered what else she could write about to grab the attention of younger singles. She thought about spring/summer romances. Her girlfriends talked incessantly about those celebrity match-ups when they went to the salons.

After about an hour pondering those writerly questions, she took a break and grabbed a drink at the bar. She hoped Raoul, the eye-candy bartender would be on duty. He was witty and entertaining to be around. She threw on her daisy dukes and headed out.

On her way to the bar she came upon a small group of guys gathered around a table overlooking the pool. Wouldn't you know it? Good old stumble-and-fall Enrique himself was in the center of the discussion. Curiously, he appeared to be holding court of some sort. She waited a minute on the side, out of sight, and listened.

Enrique said, "Guys. Listen, all your talk about women being impossible to understand is rubbish. Women are just different. That's all. You have to go with the flow and learn to listen better."

Wow, she thought to herself. *A guy who understands women. Miracles never cease to amaze. A male with a brain.*

Justin chimed in, "How do you know so much? I don't see a wedding ring on your fingers. Not to be a wise guy but you are on a singles cruise with us, right?"

"Well, yes and no." Enrique countered to both points. "To your first point, I've got other business here, and to your second point, I've been a widower for over seven years now. My wife Marilyn, God rest her soul, and I were married for twenty beautiful years. We had three kids probably your ages who are doing great now. Back then it was about listening, and it's no different now."

"I'm sorry," Justin quickly reacted, wishing he hadn't pushed back so hard at Enrique.

"Don't worry about it," said Enrique re-assuring him. "I've been dating for three or four years now but just haven't found anyone to rival my Marilyn."

The guys around Enrique seemed a bit in awe of him. They'd all had their share of relationship troubles. Enrique seemed to carry weight with the young guys. Even Fabian, often outspoken with his brusque Italian mannerisms, took a back seat to Enrique.

Tina had observed long enough. She moved past the guy's table on the pool side. Enrique caught a glimpse of her out of the corner of his eye and shouted, "Hey, Tina, come on over and meet the guys."

That wasn't part of her plan. She didn't want to be the only person in a bathing suit at a table full of guys. She turned toward Enrique and the guys as she moved past their table, smiled broadly, and said, "It's so nice of you, but I've been out in the sun too long. I'm heading over to the bar to grab a drink."

As soon as the words passed by her lips, she knew she shouldn't have mentioned a drink or the bar.

"Come on back," she heard someone in the group yell desperately. "We'll buy you a drink. You are on a singles cruise. We're all single."

It was Fabian. The guys were laughing. Tina looked back at them expressionless. Fabian caught her tone and quickly changed from his bravado gear to a false plea for mercy, saying, "Unless you think our lonely souls aren't even worth a short visit."

Tina stopped for a moment to acknowledge his unsuccessful testosterone-less campaign. She waved her hand, and said, "Nice to see you all." She locked eyes with Enrique and said, "Enrique, teach these guys some manners, will you?"

Then she turned and strutted off toward the bar with an emphatic, eye-catching, fashion-runway gait. The guys looked at Enrique with their mouths open. Their gaping expressions said it all. She had appointed Enrique to be the schoolmaster. They were his apprentices. The bar was open and set high to be with Tina.

13

Were the Cats Watching?

Raoul saw Tina approaching the bar. He was pleased to see her. He flexed his arms and gave her a big smile. They hit it off well.

"The usual?"

"Yeah," she grinned. "Sex on the Beach." A few of her earlier suitors were at the bar.

Raoul delivered a perfect drink. She sipped slowly—swirling the red straw around with her tongue. She knew she was teasing the hell out of the guys at the bar. The men threw little softballs of eye contact for her to catch. She tried to ignore them all. She had a half-hour to kill before she'd catch the elevator to the seventh below deck floor and room 713.

A friendly woman took a seat next to Tina and struck up a conversation. Joanna, a cute black woman with a nose piercing, worked for a small publishing company doing administrative work. Joanna, from LA, had high hopes to meet someone on the cruise. She loved to help writers research and organize their manuscripts. She excelled at scheduling book signings. But she wanted more in life. She hoped to eventually write herself and wanted to meet a writer.

As Joanna sipped her iced drink with Kahlua and vodka, she confessed to Tina that she didn't have a lot of confidence in finding "Mr. Right."

"The hell with Mr. Right." said Tina laughing. "But just for kicks and giggles, what would Mr. Right look like? What would he be like?" she asked as she tilted her head, pursed her lips, winked her left eye, and made her signature funny smile. It was an irresistible tease that worked on everyone—male or female.

"Well," taking the bait, Joanna started her list. "He'd have to like animals. He'd have a good job. He couldn't be fat; it just wouldn't work. And he'd want kids too."

"Really?" Tina asked in a mocking way, "Kids?"

"Yeah, I'm a family girl."

Tina doubted herself as she spoke. "I'm fine with a good-looking, athletic guy that loves to travel—no kids in the plan."

Joanna fired right back, "Really?" They both giggled. "So, tell me," Joanna continued. "What else completes your Mr. Right? What would he look like and be like?"

Tina sat for a moment, pensive and subdued. Could she articulate to Joanna the perfect man for her?

Tina looked at Raoul. He was tending bar unaware of her searching eyes and penetrating thoughts. Joanna noticed. "Uh-huh?" she said.

"What?" Tina said, soft-pedaling and somewhat annoyed.

"Uh, huh?" Joanna repeated nodding in Raoul's direction. She repeated it again, "Uh-huh."

"No, No! Raoul's just big, and he's in front of us. And well . . . big," Tina repeated.

"Uh, huh? So you are thinking of someone big. Is that it? Is that all?" Joanna murmured in a smarmy, prep-school, pretend-to-believe way.

Joanna had her claws in to the prey. She wasn't going to let this go. It was too much fun.

"Maybe you mean that you like heavy people more than skinny people?" teased Joanna.

Alright, she thought, losing patience, *I'll lay it all out there for you.* "Mr. Right needs to be independent, sexy, feisty enough to stand up to me now and then, yet peaceful inside. He has to like me for my brains—not what I look like. He must be reflective to really get ME. Now do you know what I mean?"

"There's more. He has to be energetic, but he can't be agitated all the time. And he must be kind and considerate. He has to think of others fifty-one percent of the time before he thinks of himself. He's got to know his way—and not be all over the place. And he should like yoga and cats too. And I'll throw him right out of our house if he looks at other women."

She decided to end with, "And he has to have a perfect body, and a great sense of humor too. He can't be a fun sucker!"

Tina stopped suddenly. She was surprised at how quickly she blurted all that out. They looked at each other and broke out laughing.

"What do you mean—a fun sucker?" Joanna said.

Tina responded, "You know the type of people who suck the fun out of everything. Oh . . . I hate them."

"Oh yeah," said Joanna. "I've met my share of those."

Together they had engineered a perfect comedy sketch, except it wasn't.

They had high hopes for this singles cruise. The men on the cruise did, too. The men wanted those same perfect traits and perfect bodies.

Tina and Joanna and most of their girlfriends flung themselves at exercise and diets and yoga and meditation in the hopes of being that person, finding that person—HIM, the special him.

As much fun as they were having, Tina was losing patience with Joanna's faux questioning. Joanna's questions underscored Tina's nervousness about being on a single's cruise. There was serious stuff just below the surface for most of the people on this cruise. She wasn't the only one who felt it.

Should she lower her standards? If not, would she be single forever? It was a haunting thought. She'd convinced herself that Mr. Right was out there.

Yet here she was at the pool bar sipping her favorite unwind drink and cancel-talking those very hopes. The drink settled her nerves and thoughts. She decided to let go of all those thoughts and enjoy herself.

Tina and Joanna hit it off so well. The two of them took turns making fun of the guys around the bar—French; the two gym rats, Rico and Chico. Of course, those weren't their real names, but the girls enjoyed their quirky name game. They laughed heartily as they invented new names for the men. The Green Dragon, the Eight-ball, the Bald Destroyer, Tarzan, and Boy Wonder, and myriad other heartless names. They wondered how they were being labeled too.

Tina's time had run out. She wanted to see Flora May. After a quick discussion, Joanna and Tina agreed to meet at yoga the next day. The women got up together, hugged, and were off for their respective destinations. Tina—to room 713, and Joanna to meet a deck officer for a tour of the bridge.

Joanna's friend, who had recently been on a cruise, told Joanna to make sure to get a bridge tour, so Joanna stopped by the hospitality desk in the morning and the staff person there arranged for a guided tour with one of the ship's officers.

Tina headed to the stairs to go up one level toward the nearest elevator entry. At the first step, she looked up and was surprised to see Mr. Stumble-and-Fall himself coming down the stairs, sans the Hawaiian shirt. She moved to one side and held tightly to the stair rails as he made his way down the steep, narrow, steel stairs toward her.

"Why it's you. Hello. I've got your perfume stuck on me," he said cheerily, "and I wouldn't want it any other way."

Tina couldn't help but smile, although she remained guarded.

"I was hoping to run into you. I'd love to get together with you. Maybe we could get a drink or take a walk on the upper deck—enjoy the view. What do you think?"

Tina exhaled what she hoped was an inaudible sigh. Enrique presented a unique challenge to her. He was an interesting guy, feisty and very sure of himself—but the age bridge—Geez. She didn't want to date anyone her father's age.

Still, other than the Hawaiian shirt, he seemed to have some class. She thought about the things she described to Joanna about her Mr. Right. She hadn't found him before the cruise—that's for sure. Maybe she was looking in the wrong places.

She wondered if she should give Enrique a chance.

He took her hesitation for a yes, and said, "Good. It's settled then. I'll see you after yoga for some fresh air."

She wondered what Flora May would think of her "chance" meeting. Were the cats watching?

14

Cute Old Guy or Just Old?

Enrique and Tina decided to meet at the small café on the port side of the ship. Enrique got to the café early and picked a table in a shaded spot in the corner. He waved Tina over. Tina was in a good mood. She decided to challenge Enrique and see what he was made of. What could it hurt? She'd give him a smile if nothing else. Maybe some karma would swing back to her.

She looked straight into his eyes and pointedly asked, "Tell me why I should spend any time at all with you. If I got close to you, you might even knock me right into the ocean if I got anywhere near the ship's rail."

Enrique responded, "Really. That's how you want to start. Perhaps you should convince me why I should spend my time with you."

Their interaction was starting to be fun. *Great*, Enrique thought. *She's sassy.* That was on his list for Mrs. Right. She had to be someone who was playful and spontaneous. She had to be young at heart. There were plenty of older boring women for him to meet. He had no patience for older women who acted their age. It was quite unfair but that was how he felt.

After his ridiculous clumsiness on the forward deck, he wondered if he'd get a chance to let her know who he was and find out if she had similar thoughts.

This was his opportunity. Enrique, warmed by her friendly tone, thought to himself, *Say something smart.* He'd been over it in his head one hundred times. He wanted to say something that would impress her but was dumbfounded in the moment. Instead, he said the first thing that popped in his head.

"Did I see you coming out of 713 earlier this week?"

He hoped it didn't seem like he was stalking her. His job made him ultra-observant.

"Yeah" said Tina, "I saw Flora May, the fortune teller. Did you see her?"

"No, I'm more of a goal-setter than a fate and fortune guy."

More self-doubt. He thought to himself, *You dumb-ass — you just made fun of her fortune telling visit. She probably loves that stuff.*

"You seemed very good at yoga. Do you do yoga often?"

She thought to herself, *This guy sure asks a lot of questions. Maybe he is a stalker? I hope not.*

She responded to his question, "Yeah, I try to do yoga three or four times a week. It helps me stay grounded."

Small talk wasn't Enrique's strong suit, especially with attractive women like Tina. He thought to himself: *Just tell her she's beautiful and that you like her sassiness.* That turned into, "You are pretty smart with all that sassiness."

Oh . . . geez that came out wrong, he thought to himself. He frowned as if he just burned himself on a hot stove, and thought, *That's the wrong tone. No wonder I have trouble with women. I'm not good at this.*

Tina took it all in stride. "Enrique, you seem stressed. Is everything okay?" She clearly was amused by his discomfort.

For his part, what he really wanted to share was who he was. Not his age, not his wit, but what his experience could mean to her.

He shot back, "I'm only as confused as everyone else in this matrix you women make."

"Really," Tina fired back. "We don't make the matrix. Love needs balance, like two people on a seesaw. But you men always lean too heavily."

Enrique disagreed. He watched couples for years trying to fix and control their partners—especially the women. Enrique figured people had to fix their own stuff, or not, by themselves. He was pretty sure this wasn't the time to stake that claim.

He'd lean as light as he could if Tina would play the game, but it didn't sound like that was going to happen.

Enrique's thoughts had collided with her thoughts enough for one day. He decided to back down and take a pass. He thought to himself, *If it's meant to be, it will be.*

She made him a nervous wreck.

Enrique finally found his words, "You know, when I was young, I'd find somebody and we'd come together in a relationship. And when things went wrong, I'd try to fix that person, or change them. I didn't work enough on myself. It was like looking through a telescope backwards," he said. "It's funny. I repeated that whole process multiple times. It was both comical and fruitless. I'd make trade-offs to keep those people in my life. I don't do that anymore."

Tina tilted her ear toward him to encourage him to go on. Enrique made sense to her.

"The older place I'm at is a place that muscles and perfect bodies can't take you. If that's a place you'd like to go, then maybe let's take that walk I asked you for."

He took a breath and waited. She thought for a minute about how unusual the truth he shared with her was. He was down to earth, obviously—but not obvious to most people, and before this conversation, not even obvious to her that those sentiments would come from Enrique.

She found herself responding with uncharacteristic sarcasm, "Yeah. Okay. After yoga, we'll grab coffee and take a walk. But we won't walk so far as to stress your fatigued old body! And we'll stay away from the outside rail too."

He smiled to himself as if he had made some big achievement. It was. It had been a significant task to try and overcome his social awkwardness, and his own bias. His trip and fall earlier had evidenced his lack of confidence when he was with her. It contradicted his usually unflappable business persona. Facing this part of himself was more unsettling than he cared to admit.

Each time she responded, he was pleasantly surprised and intrigued by her gamesmanship. They had a connection. He got that "inside smile" we all get when we recognize that we like someone more than we thought we would. Tina had that "inside smile" too. She smiled at him, and in her moment of innocence, he caught a glimpse of her inside smile too. He wondered how much he should tell her about himself.

15

Surprises All Around

Yoga finished and Tina caught Enrique's eye from the back of the Yoga area. He walked over toward her, careful not to trip—very careful. He wanted desperately to change her first impression of him.

"Hi, Tina, how did you like the yoga?

Tina replied, "It was great. I still can't remember the names of the positions though—so I kind of fake it until I see what everyone else is doing. How about you?"

Laughing he replied, "Sure, it's great fun if you think turning yourself into a pretzel is a fun way to spend a morning."

Tina teased back "It wasn't that bad."

Enrique fired back, "Oh, yes, it was that bad. But at least it has given me an excuse to talk to you. Tell me about yourself. Is pretzel-making yoga your only thing?" he asked teasingly.

Tina wasn't used to sharing her story first. Most of the men she dated talked a lot about themselves. Their stories always came first.

For some strange reason, she decided to not hold back and tell Enrique about herself.

"I come from Georgia. I like yoga and cats. I work in insurance and I'm trying to start a writing career."

Enrique knew about her writing. He had seen her article in "Travel The World In Style" magazine. He was probably one of only a few people on board who had read it. Enrique's son was the managing editor of that magazine. Enrique read all of the articles in that magazine—every month. He thought her article about travel as a single person was a good one.

Enrique listened carefully to her response, not yet ready to divulge his connection or that he knew she was an aspiring writer. He was interested in knowing more about her.

He asked, "Do you like being single? I've heard all kinds of viewpoints. I'd love to hear your take on it."

"Wow," Tina said, delaying her response for a moment to let the question sink in. "I'm not sure I'm ready to handle that question."

He laughed and said, "It's one of the matrix questions."

Smart Ass. As she thought about her answer, she walked over toward the Painted Turtle bar and picked out a deck lounge chair. He followed. She set the back of the chair at a sixty-percent incline and motioned Enrique to join her with the chair beside hers.

One of the deck waiters stopped by and asked if they wanted a drink. Tina said, "Sure. Could I get a mocha coffee and it'd be great if you had a chocolate stick to dip into the coffee?"

"Yes, Ma'am." said the waiter. "What room number?"

She hesitated for a moment before deciding it was okay that Enrique knew her room number. Women with Tina's looks had good reason to be guarded. "Room C-111" She didn't see the harm in letting Enrique hear her room number. By this point, she was sure he wasn't a threat.

Enrique took note, quietly storing her room number in his "Tina vault." He didn't need the number to find her. His position on board gave him access to most of the ship's data.

As she sat with Enrique, the phrase "sugar daddy" crept into her thoughts. Tina couldn't help herself. She hated that whole "age thing" and all the celebrity-style dogma that surrounded it.

Enrique looked at her young, lithe figure and the "sugar daddy" phrase popped into his head too. He wondered about their age difference and what effect it might have should they get to the next stage. He didn't know her age, but he guessed she was twenty years younger than himself.

He wondered whether he should bring it up. He couldn't know that she was thinking the very same thoughts. He decided it was too early to bring it up. They hadn't gotten to "there"—to discuss that indelicate subject just yet. They might never get there—so why waste time when they could just chat and enjoy each other's company. Those early awkward moments in relationships are hard enough to overcome without chasing dreams and adding trouble.

By now, he knew he was attracted to Tina. It was a strong attraction. He didn't expect that. That wasn't part of his travel plans for this cruise. But his stumble two days ago, and her perfume had sent a laser beacon to his heart—or maybe it was one of Sheila's Cupid arrows. The "Joys of Love" cruise director was really good at her job.

He found himself attuned to Tina's every move when he was near her. Tina reminded Enrique of a girl he met skiing in the Alps in Northern Italy years ago. He even remembered the name of her perfume—Elegance. That fit Tina well.

For Tina's part, Enrique represented intrigue. No one knew much about him. She'd never thought of herself as being with someone too much older than herself. It was taboo to her independent soul—or so she thought. She would never be dependent on anyone, much less someone older than herself.

She questioned herself, we all think we're so damn independent. But are we?

Enrique re-issued his question, "Do you like being single?"

It was a sincere question. He was single by choice, but not always happy about it.

"You are single, aren't you? Tina replied in her best curious, puzzle-solving way.

Sensing he might have crossed a line, Enrique back stepped, "Ah, I'm not saying there's anything wrong with being single. It's just that I've grappled with being single for, I don't know, an extended period of time."

"Oh, so you are lonely?" responded Tina. Tina expected one of those manly denials. Enrique thought about her prod and said, "Well, to be honest, yeah. I'm lonely, but not all the time. But maybe on a date night when I don't have a date."

"I see," said Tina taking an inquisitive, reflective stance.

She waited to let him add—to tease him out.

It was a waiting game for the two of them. They could feel the tension. The connection was there but they couldn't quite bridge their gap—not yet.

They decided to continue their walk on the aft section of the boat. Tina thought they could do a lap and get her step count up.

Enrique didn't want her to think he wasn't up to the pace and stayed just ahead of her as they circled the deck. Truthfully, he would have rather been behind her. It's a man thing.

When they arrived back to the Painted Turtle and their chairs, Enrique decided to cross the "sugar daddy" bridge.

16

The Sugar Daddy Bridge

Enrique, as was his habit in life, went head on into the issue. "So what do you think of spring/summer romances?"

Tina didn't blush. She smiled to herself. *Alright, he's put it all out there. What should I do? Avoid. That's what.*

She needed to know more about him. From her earlier conversation, she got the sense that he was into computers. She was getting a clear signal that there was a lot more to Enrique than meets the eye.

Avoiding the sugar daddy question, she continued, "So, tell me about you and your work. What do you do?"

"Well, now I'm more of an investor and a manager. For several years I was a software designer for a toy company. We made videos that helped us sell our toys."

"Oh, that seems interesting," said Tina.

"Sometimes yes. Sometimes not so much. It was often a royal pain, frankly."

"Oh, I wouldn't have thought that. What makes it so difficult?"

Enrique found Tina to be a good conversationalist, better than he expected. Her good looks held an old bias with him. He thought most good-looking women were dumb-asses. There! He said it out loud—sort of, to himself. Clearly he was surprised with her conversational skills- for no other reason than because she was good looking.

And clearly in her case, his bias was unfounded.

He continued, "I think every job has its challenges. It's probably me. It's just such a paradigm. You do all this sophisticated computer work to tease young kids into begging their parents for toys. From that perspective, it's not very fulfilling—even if it was financially rewarding."

"Well, I can see that," said Tina. "But there's lots of different ways to look at it. Providing jobs, enriching kids' imaginations, encouraging kids to know computers. Who knows where a child's brain can go once you inspire them?"

Everything Tina said drew him closer to her. He actually felt shivers up his spine when he thought about her complimentary comments. It had been a while since he'd been around someone so positive and engaging.

"Where do you work?" she asked.

"For several years, I worked out of San Diego and I have a second office in Malpensa, Italy, near the airport," said Enrique. "But I often travel to Mexico. That's where I get my inspiration."

"Oh, what part of Mexico?" asked Tina.

Could she know Mexico? he wondered. He mentioned Monterrey.

Tina's eyes lit up, "I love Monterrey. I've been there twice. It's so modern! They do such a great job with tile design in the public buildings there."

Damn, he thought to himself, *this is crazy. She even likes Mexico.* It was one of his favorite travel destinations.

As they talked, Tina's youthful persona made him feel his age.

Enrique didn't like the thought of being a sugar daddy, probably more than Tina resented the term. It made him feel old. Well maybe he was old—certainly compared to her.

In his heart, though, he was young. He wondered how he could show her. He wanted her to know that he wasn't, well, jilted with an old man's view; that he had the energy and ideas of someone much younger.

In the back of Tina's mind, she could hear her grandmother— her mostly crazy grandmother, telling her, "Go for the money sweetheart. Love is overrated!"

Of course, Tina's mom would have no part of that advice. In one of her lectures, her mom tersely reminded Tina of how her "crazy-as-a-graham-cracker" grandmother had run off with a minor league baseball player, leaving her first husband inconsolable.

The whole family disowned Graham-Cracker-Granny until she met and married Tina's grandfather.

As Tina milled over those anecdotes, Ricky (her dancing buddy), jogged by them and pulled up quickly when he saw Tina.

"Oh, my love. Are you dancing with me tonight?" Tina shut her eyes for a moment, not sure what to say.

Enrique took care of it. "We'll both be there tonight. See you there, shorty."

It left his mouth. He felt bad. It was the opposite of the image he wanted to convey, and the opposite of who he was. Tina had a strong effect on him—too strong. He was aggravated with himself.

Ricky didn't seem to mind. He cheerily waved and kept running. Enrique observed Tina's face. She grimaced and quickly erased it from her face. He hoped he hadn't squelched her response or made her uncomfortable by usurping Ricky's invitation to her.

He noticed his social ineptness jumped to a new level when he was near Tina.

He hoped he didn't look like a giant dumb-ass. Tina looked at him. His lips were pinched together with a remorseful expression. Tina waited a moment and decided to put Enrique at ease and added, "Okay. Great! We'll have fun. That's why we're here."

Enrique's face relaxed. Ricky and the whole question of sugar daddy would have to wait.

The dance floor would be busy.

17

The Devil in a White Uniform

Joanna came out of her room on the second night of their cruise into the dimly lit, narrow corridor. Round overhead lights about every five feet were lit so poorly you couldn't tell they had a bulb. The hallway looked like an airport runway on low batteries. The rooms were staggered on each side of the hall. The door numbers were shiny brass which helped illuminate the number so you could at least determine your room. As she traced back her steps to the bar where she met the deck officer an hour earlier, she turned a corner and bumped right into him. That was a surprise, at least to her.

Ken wore a close-fit white, short-sleeved shirt with two bars on his right sleeve. A breast pocket held a tiny spiral notebook and two pens. The front pocket hosted a medic pin. He pulled the notebook out and jotted down her name at the bar. She thought that was odd but found a way that it made sense so she wouldn't worry.

Very industrious, she thought; Top officer material for sure.

For his part Ken liked the ladies. He was soft on the eyes with boyish blond hair, blue eyes, and a Scandinavian build—tall and thin-chested. Slightly puffy cheeks made for an easy smile. He knew his smile looked great. He practiced it all the time. He looked in the mirror a full fifteen minutes every day. His face was irresistible. All you had to do to know that was ask him.

Ken liked the way Joanna looked—spicy—maybe a rule breaker. Like him. From where he sat, he could tell she had a nice, robust top.

He decided to check out her bottom. He didn't want to alert her to what he was up to, so he avoided eye contact. He went round the bar the long way to the head to check her out.

Joanna wore a mini-skirt with fish-net stockings. Oh yeah! He was interested.

She wore a soft orange camisole over a tight, thin melon-col-ored T-shirt. It was a perfect match. She was a perfect match for him. As he made his way back to his seat across the bar, he framed his face with his perfect smile and shot her a glance. If she caught it, he'd pull out his imaginary lasso gun and fish the line back.

As luck would have it, she tilted her head to scan the bar, stop-ping for just a second too long as she found him. Got it, he thought. He nodded his head, just like he did in the mirror each day. It was the tiniest nod. You had to look hard to see it.

Ken kept tapping and snapping and mouthing the words. The song was almost over. He tilted his head and gave her a friendly nod and smirch. She grinned back. Mistake one for her; point for him.

Alright, he thought to himself. She's ready for step two—a little friendly banter, a shoulder touch with his fingers as swooped in to hear her talk.

This time as he headed around the bar, he went the shorter, more direct way—maybe nine chairs away; two empties, four guys, and three other women. The first one was too old, He couldn't do her. The second one, not fat, but please take care of yourself, lady. The third was doable but he hadn't gotten the signal from her yet. Maybe tomorrow. His gunslinger mentality had served him well. He knew all the food types and how to approach each.

This one needed a soft touch. No fast-talking. Meander over to her chair.

Bring the boyish grin.

"Hi! What's happening over at your end of the bar?"

Should have added, beautiful—but didn't. Damn, I'm slipping, he thought.

"I was getting a little lonely, but then I saw you—beautiful, or rather stunning—I should say."

Oh, a player, Joanna thought. Her first "Out." She was right but somehow she talked herself out of that too.

She convinced herself that he had a great way about him—easily complimenting others. It would be a treat to be with someone special who cared about others.

Before she knew it, he had laid his arm on her shoulder and started tracing tiny circles above her elbow. Light touch, very light touch, very small circles. Joanna liked that. Woof. She was getting hot.

Joanna leaned her head into his arm. She wondered if he could tell.

It wasn't so hard to tell. He prided himself in picking up those signals from women—even older women. He caught on quickly and rolled his wrist against her breast, very lightly, just a hint of soft touch.

Gunslinger was a cad. In fact, a real jerk. He kept a Rolodex of his friend's mothers too. He considered himself an honorary member of the "MILF" club. He'd try to score on each of his friend's moms with a boyish charm, but then adding a thick "schtick" of unapologetic sexy compliments like, "You've got really great breasts. I like the way older women move their hips. You are so much more experienced than the young girls I meet."

For Joanna, those compliments made fireworks go off with that sound-searing whistle that trails at the end. Of course, gunslinger Ken held a blow torch to the fireworks display with his hand behind his back.

He reached in with his other hand to her lap. She jolted, and he pulled back immediately. That was her second "out."

Did she know? No. How could she?

"Can I buy you a drink? I bet you'd like a silk-panty martini."

It was his second tell. She blushed but accepted it.

"I'll have a beer," he told the bartender.

"You got it, bro!"

Her third "out" was right there in front of her. She just couldn't see it.

Ken was ready for the banter next. He was good at it.

"So who is your favorite actor?"

"I like goofy comedies. Like the Eddy Murphy ones—bit of slapstick with a message."

"No, really. Mine too!"

She remembered the movie with the animals and Murphy's voice.

"I loved that movie."

Whoa, she thought, my dream guy not only existed, but is right here in front of me.

He must be "the one." Where else would we meet, she thought to herself. We're on a cruise designed for love. And she loved how he snapped his fingers to the beat of her favorite song, "Sweet Caroline." Earlier when she first sat down and watched him from across the bar, she noticed one hand tapped and the other snapped. Eyes half shut, mouthing the words. Tapping and snapping. Perfect!

"Sweet Caroline"—the perfect Boston song. She was from LA. It was taboo. Boston fans and LA fans competed on every level, especially sports but even in entertainment. Back in the day, Magic vs. Bird, then Pierce vs. Lebron, the Red Sox vs. the Dodgers.

Her friends just couldn't forgive her for being such a renegade.

But she was. And she knew it. She loved to buck the system, wherever she went.

And there HE was tapping and snapping and mouthing the words she loved.

He got her name and actually wrote it down. That showed something about him. He wouldn't allow himself to forget her name.

She'd had two drinks and knew herself. She had to cool her jets so she stalled him a bit, and said that she had to call her mom. She wasn't—not then anyways. It was too late back home. Mom went to bed early.

So they smiled and agreed to meet in the morning when he got off duty.

She was really surprised when she bumped into him coming back from her room. He wasn't surprised. As she headed out—not too close to seem like he was following her, he quickly phoned a buddy to check the ship's log. It was no accident he got to her corridor. He had Joanna's name and got her room number from his buddy. He was on his way.

She was a little tipsy. It didn't take much convincing—smooth as he was.

In the morning he'd point his index finger at the mirror with his thumb up, and make believe shoot—making a little sound "bang, bang." Ken would surely notch another bullet—a big mirror smile tomorrow, he thought to himself—as he came upon her around the corner. He measured his prey quickly. He'd appear a little startled but give her a big smile instantly. It was going to be easy.

The devil didn't always wear red. This time the devil wore a crisp white uniform.

18

An Unexpected Meeting for the Gunslinger

Joanna got up early. She felt great. She couldn't wait to meet up with Mr. Right again. She ripped into her exercise routine. She had on her tightest shorts. She loved to dress up, especially for someone special.

When she came up to the fifth deck, where he mentioned his main station was, she saw him and immediately ran over. "Ken, Ken, how are you this morning, my love?"

He looked up at her with dread. Under his breath, he said, "Oh shit!"

"Yeah, Hi. I'm working now and don't have time."

"When will you be off?" she asked.

"Hard to say. Maybe not for two more days. Last night was my first time off in a week. I don't have any time." He was merciless.

He eeked out a half-ass "Sorry," turned and walked away.

She wanted to say, "You son of a bitch. You will be sorry!" But she couldn't force a single word out. There wasn't anything she could do. She didn't really think she could make him sorry. She brought it on herself and she knew it.

Joanna stumbled away from him; her joyful run to him stopped in its tracks as if a train had run her over or a bullet had gone right through her.

Now she had to call her mom. This was worse than embarrassing. She'd been used. She knew it. Gunslinger Ken had another notch in his belt—and she was it.

She felt like shit.

She was crying by the time she phoned her mom, but she tried to hold back.

She dreaded the call because she knew what her mom would say, what her mom was thinking—even before her mom said it—or thought it. But she was crushed; she had to call. It hurt so much.

"Ma, it's me."

The response came instantly, "What is it honey? There's something wrong isn't there. Are you okay? What's going on there? Tell me. Tell me, sweetheart."

Moms know. Just two seconds into the call and her mom knew. Joanna wondered how she would tell her. All those lectures sped into her brain. You know what men want. Don't give them anything. You've got to know someone before you commit. Don't be a slut!

Ohhh. She dreaded the call. Her mom wouldn't say those words to her, but she knew those thoughts rolled around in both of their heads.

At some point, she had to accept her own stupidity. Jesus, she hated these kind of moments. When you know you've done something completely stupid and you can't take it back. The cheap feeling.

"Mom. Don't tell Dad."

"I know, honey. Don't worry."

Her mom thought to herself—careful not to share. What the hell was her daughter thinking—going on a singles cruise? The good ones wouldn't need to be on a singles cruise.

Joanna was miserable. They reading each other's minds. It was a telepathic nightmare.

"Mom, what should I do?"

"Well first, you're okay, right?"

"He didn't hit you, did he?"

"No, Mom."

"Good!"

"What about protection?

Joanna didn't want to answer her mom. She rumbled a sigh through her vibrating lips.

"No, Mom. I didn't need it. It's my period."

"Thank the LORD!" her mother exclaimed. "Get tested any-way—in a month or so, okay?"

Just too exhausted to fight, Joanna said, "Yeah, okay."

This was a low point for Joanna. She fumed. *Fucking men. Where the hell was this guy's mother? How could he be so mean? Buying me drinks. Obviously he was trying to get me drunk so he could take advantage of me. And I let him. Jesus!*

She remembered a really tough time when her dad lost his job and her family had to go to the food bank. Her dad told her back then, "We don't always know why God sends us trials. But we know he wouldn't give them to us if we couldn't handle it. We only get as much as we can handle."

Well, Joanna had enough.

She again remembered her dad's words of advice. "One step at a time, we'll figure it out," he'd say.

So what was the next step? After another giant asshole in her life?

"Mom, I don't know what to do," Joanna cried.

"It's okay. It's okay. It's okay. It'll work out. It always does. God will help."

Joanna didn't like God very much at this point in her life. She certainly didn't want to hear from her mom just how much God was going to take care of things. She had made a mess. There was no one to blame but herself. God didn't do this.

"Mom. Thank you. I think I need to get some rest. I'll call you as soon as I wake up. I promise. Double-double promise."

19

Taut Hips on a Busy Dance Floor

Enrique could dance. Tina was in for a surprise. Ricky was younger than Enrique—as much as fifteen years younger. She had seen Ricky dance. Ooh-lah-lah.

What was Enrique going to be like out on the dance floor?

Sheila, the activity director on the cruise, was busy behind the scenes. She wanted everyone to couple up. She was a romantic from Nebraska in the Midwest. Her parents were die-hard corn-huskers and church-goers. Her view: You meet. You fall in love. You marry. You have kids. You grow old together. You die happy.

We all know it just isn't that way, except in the old movies or in short lives. Real life is a million miles from that. Even Sheila knew that. Yet in her heart, no one should leave the "Joys of Love" without getting a chance to experience love with all its passion—at least once. That was her stated goal for every cruise. Pure and passionate love for everyone.

In team meetings Sheila besieged all of her cohorts, "I want all my peeps to fall in love. You guys have to help me! It's for LOVE!"

Privately she wondered what pure love really meant. Did it mean attachment to a special someone who mirrored everything about yourself? That seemed narcissistic. She hoped love was more than that. Could love be some sort of boundless energy that enveloped the universe to heal and make things right? She hoped so. So many things were messed up. The world needed healing—badly.

Sheila's role model on board the ship was Marietta, the sous chef. Marietta restored calm with every step she took. Marietta knew how to get things done. She never seemed to let the outside world affect her. Marietta reminded Sheila of her own dad. If something needed fixing, she mentioned it to her dad, and "poof"—it got done.

Sheila's dad knew everyone in her hometown. He'd swing by the hardware store, grab a part, chat up the plumbers and the other contractors there. Then he'd come home and fix the toilet, or the faucet, or the screen, or the door, or the outlet, or the appliance that was broken.

It was that unassailable "can-do" that made Marietta's kitchen and staff run like clockwork. Sheila noticed how the Captain responded when Marietta talked. He knew the value his ship of well-prepared foods delivered with precision. The ship's restaurants didn't promise coffee and fill-belly from a local diner. Cruises were all about the best food on the planet. Guests expected that; the

Captain expected it too. He appreciated the people who made that happen.

Sheila backed Marietta and Georgio's requests for exotic menu items like rare blue lobsters or Black Sea oysters. She enlisted Marietta's help when she'd ask for her own expensive sheer chiffon fabrics for a dress-up activity she concocted.

She'd ask Marietta, "Wouldn't it be great if all the men had top-hats and the women had pink umbrellas for the send-off dinner?" Marietta knew Sheila wasn't just floating an idea. Sheila saw the whole dinner in her mind. She needed Marietta's help to squeeze the budget for another romantic splash. Marietta thought often, *To be young again—with Sheila's energy.* And then Marietta would say, "That sounds great!" to encourage Sheila.

Of course, Marietta would help Sheila. She'd give the wink to the Captain. Her own soft heart loved the energy only Sheila could bring. If hearts could smile, Sheila could make that happen.

Upon hearing of Sheila's next romantic scheme, the team would look at each other and roll their eyes. Marietta would smile and nod, sitting next to Georgio—opposite the Captain. The crew never knew what Sheila was cooking up or how Sheila got things approved and done.

The purser would look at the line items and try to say "no" as frequently as he could. But the Captain would usually just tilt his head sideways, eyeing Marietta out of the corner of his eye, make a funny cross-eyed downward glance, and say "Just make her happy, will ya?" His voice trailed away in faux exasperation. The team leaders ended up mumbling more often than not as they watched the ritual play out time and again.

Yet they all had to admit, Sheila could throw a party like no one else. And the guests loved the parties.

Everyone seemed to tug on Sheila's heartstrings—no matter what their story was. Whether it was the childhood sweethearts who came on the last cruise to get married, but ended up imploding when the groom got drunk and got caught with a bridesmaid, or an older couple on their umpteenth anniversary.

Sheila embraced them all. After all, she had played into a romantic dream with her own Mr. Right. That dream turned into a nightmare quickly. She found love years ago on this very cruise ship. That almost-perfect love was dashed by fate. Her lover found her, was with her first. But then, he turned out to be gay. That ended her dream—but it didn't cancel that dream for everyone else. Sheila would do her best to bring love into her guests' lives.

Her own disappointment made her more determined to give guests the dream she missed. She reasoned that everyone needed love or at least a chance. For Sheila, the ship was a highway of chances to romantic heaven. That's why her guests were there; to catch love in the air, that shiver of excitement one gets when a person "gets you" and shows it. She breathed in for a moment and thought back to her first night with her lover, "Ah, romantic love!" she thought to herself.

Fortunately for Tina, her romantic dream wouldn't suffer Sheila's fate. Enrique wasn't gay. That wasn't Enrique's surprise. She thought about how confident Enrique had been. She envisioned dancing with him. He'd effortlessly spin her like a top on the dance floor. She could see herself circling back into his arms—even swooning as she was caught. It would be so different from the average guy.

Most guys she had known hated the dance floor. You'd have to drag them up there. They didn't have two left feet—they had seventeen of them. They were childish babies when it came to dancing. They wouldn't sacrifice their masculine egos for fear of what?

She and her girlfriends ended up dancing with each other. The men would talk sports and other meaningless rubbish. The girls didn't care. They wanted to dance.

Sheila smartly had plans for guys that couldn't dance and guys that could. Sheila had the dance floor set up with heart balloons and soft lighting. In the corner, with their back to the sunset, the on-board band streamed out delightful salsa music.

At Sheila's cue, the band would switch to slow-dance music, then alternate to country western love ballads. She made it easy for the non-dancing guys, if only they'd have some balls.

Enrique was serious about Tina. He had spent the previous afternoon working on a song to impress her. He had written poems and ballads since he was a teenager and stored them in a little chest he kept in his closet back home.

He wanted the sounds of the song he wrote to match his feelings for Tina. He tapped out the beat as he polished up the lyrics.

You are not the one—you are all three for me,
My soul, my dreams, my love you to see,
Were I to be the lucky one for you,
Our souls would mate, my dreams come true.

And when I wished upon the stars
I'd thank them for the things you are.

He had a plan. He'd hand over his music to the band as he came onto the floor.

Tina had given her dance night some thought as well. She picked out a cute yellow and pink summer dress that she found at a consignment shop. She loved to shop at those in-town shops. This one came from a thrift shop in St. Maarten. Her budget couldn't afford for her to buy clothes in designer retail shops.

She had a good eye for what fit her thin frame. She added a rose-filled, white scarf and yellow earrings to her outfit. She checked herself in the mirror. What's missing? A belt? A bag? Ahhh . . . her big, yellow-framed, fun, sunglasses. Perfect. She headed upstairs to the dance.

Joanna Was Crying

Things didn't go as planned. As Tina left her room, she bumped into Joanna. Joanna was crying. Tina stopped to console her. "What's wrong?"

Joanna shut her eyes and grimaced in pain. "I can't. I can't talk now," she said. Her voice was staggered with sobs and sniffles.

"Well, come on back in my room," said Tina. "We'll make it right."

"No. You are supposed to be going to the dance to meet that older guy, right?"

"He can wait," said Tina. "Tell me what happened."

Tina ushered Joanna into her room and encouraged her to sit on the bed.

"Well, you remember that bridge tour I took with that cute officer from Florida? It went too well—if you know what I mean. It was my fault. I let it. That's how men are, right?"

"Wait. Wait. What do you mean? What happened? Did he hurt you?"

"No. No. Well, yeah. After."

"What do you mean?" said Tina as she grabbed a tissue and handed it to Joanna. Joanna tried to remember exactly what transpired. It was like a dream; a dream gone terribly badly.

Tina thought back to her own giant mistake with a local cop back home. He had been an acquaintance, someone she had dated in high school. One night, after a chance meeting at a supermarket, they went to his apartment. Things went a little too far. She couldn't stop him. It changed everything for her. But not for him.

She changed jobs and changed towns. Somehow she didn't get pregnant. Not then, and not ever since then.

Joanna interrupted Tina's thoughts. Tina zoomed back to the present.

"Well," Joanna continued, "we ended up in his room, and . . . you know."

"No, I don't understand," Tina said. "Slow down. Please tell me exactly what happened."

Joanna took a deep breath and looked at the crumpled tissue in her hand.

"I saw him in the corridor the very next day after we . . . after we . . . " She stopped in mid-sentence. She couldn't say the words. In Joanna's mind, the rapture of their moment turned to vulgarity in an instant when he brushed by her in the hallway without saying a word. He didn't even nod or say hello. "He brushed by me, like he didn't even know me. I was crushed."

Tina knew exactly what she meant. She even knew the guy. Where was Moonlight? Moonlight should have done some better claw work on Florida boy.

They talked for a while and slowly Joanna pulled herself together. The women decided to clean up their tears and smudged make-up and go to the dance floor together.

Enrique had waited patiently for Tina. When she came out of the elevator with Joanna he was surprised that she had a guest, but happy to see her. He beckoned them over to his table.

"So this is your friend. Nice to meet you. You must be . . ."

"Joanna," she said, as she extended her hand. "Pleased to meet you."

"Can I buy you girls a drink?"

"Yeah, we could sure use one," said Tina.

Enrique knew something wasn't right. His plan for Tina would have to wait. Enrique carried on with small talk with the two women. He wondered how he might help. He'd find out soon enough.

21

Enrique Didn't Like the News

It didn't take long for the news to spill out. Enrique could tell from Joanna's make-up and something about how the two women clung together at that moment. Something was awry. He made it his business to find out what happened.

Joanna was obviously distressed. He could see sadness and even desperation in her eyes. He didn't know why. She knew. She was disgusted with herself and the ship's "gunslinger" officer.

Enrique had the soul of a shaman priest. His way of reaching out to Joanna was amazing to watch. It was one of his gifts. Back home people always came to Enrique to spill. He could lift mountains off of shoulders. Friends always came to him and felt better after a heart-to-heart chat. They either knew just what to do after meeting, or they waited for Enrique to make one of his classic magic fixes.

"Joanna, Joanna, Joanna." He spoke deliberately to get her attention. He always repeated his daughter's name three times when she was distressed. She always curled up with him when she heard her dad's "three calls" for attention.

"Did you know I have two daughters? Maria Victoria, my oldest, and Gabriella, my youngest. You might even be her age. She's twenty-one. We call her Gaby for short. At any rate, she recently had some man trouble and to be honest, you remind me exactly of that."

Joanna looked at him, both curious and suspicious.

He continued, "That's not the pretty face I saw at the bar, now is it? Would it be okay for you to share a little of your trouble with an experienced father-type like me?"

Enrique locked in to her tear-filled eyes. His pupils didn't move or shift at all. They searched. He'd seen those sad eyes from his daughter Gaby several times before. He wondered: *Why the tears? It couldn't be that bad, could it?*

"Well I'm not sure if I should say anything," said Joanna.

Tina chimed in, "He's okay. Maybe he can help. I trust him."

Tina didn't know why she trusted Enrique. She wondered if she should have so openly supported him. But he was so sincere. She could tell he wanted to help. And he had daughters.

After a deep breath, Joanna continued, "Well, I was at the bar just relaxing and unwinding." She stopped to let out a sob before she continued.

"This guy, the ship's medic I think, came over to check in on me. I think he checks in on everyone on the cruise," Joanna continued, still showing her naivete. "He looked so official. He had a silver medic pin on his pocket and two stripes on each sleeve. And he was handsome too."

Enrique listened to Joanna's every syllable, every breath with compassion. He didn't let a single thought of his own enter his mind. He focused solely on her and what she had to say. He lowered his voice as he encouraged Joanna to share the whole story.

"Yes, yes. Keep going. Then what?"

Tears were in her eyes. More tears were coming. Her cheeks dampened. Tina reached over with a tissue.

Joanna's voice parched as she struggled to clear her throat. Joanna clutched the tissue, dried her eyes, gulped and continued.

"His name was Ken something. I didn't get his last name," she said, sniffling throughout.

Enrique knew Ken's last name wasn't offered. The man wouldn't have told her, so Enrique made note of the officer's first name—Ken.

Most of the ship's passengers didn't understand the hierarchy on a ship, and how a ship operated. Nor did they know what this event might mean to a Captain. Enrique did.

Owning his own businesses for years, Enrique knew the seriousness of the incident. Besides, he had already spent time with the Captain. They talked boats, destinations they'd both visited, and leadership. It was Enrique's favorite topic.

Enrique's demeanor changed upon hearing the details of Joanna's story. He guessed quickly how Ken came upon Joanna after she left the bar that evening. Joanna hadn't put two and two together. Enrique wouldn't tell her at this point. It wouldn't help.

Enrique knew exactly what Ken had done as soon as he heard Joanna mention her "surprising" encounter with Ken in the hallway just a few minutes after she left the bar.

Enrique was distressed by the story, both as a friend and as a father and as a business owner, and quite simply as a person. And he knew his friend, the Captain, needed to hear this story.

Enrique went from playful and ready to socialize on the dance floor with Tina to rock-solid angry and motivated on Joanna's behalf. He knew what to do.

First he'd verify the story. He'd check all the likely sources. He reached out to the cruise ship's activity director, the bartender, and the sous chef who knew all the inner workings of the ship. They all had good hearts and BIG ears on board the ship.

After Joanna settled a bit from telling her story, Tina, Joanna, and Enrique tried to relax as they shared a bottle of Merlot and ordered some scallops wrapped in bacon from the hors d'oeuvres menu. They all moved slowly through the rest of the evening. The storybook contest dance with a winner-take-all ending was cancelled.

When Enrique got up to leave, the women hugged. Enrique made his way quickly to his destination—the bridge.

Tina was more curious than ever about Enrique. He seemed really determined when he got up and headed away from the table. He seemed to be on a mission. She wondered what he was up to. Her curiosity was piqued. She wanted more than ever to find out about her secretive new friend.

She decided to follow him. She didn't think it was wrong to see where he went. But she was a little edgy about following him. What would he think if he found out?

She stayed about fifty feet behind him until he got into the elevator. It was the center elevator that went to the bridge. She could tell from the indicator lights that the elevator stopped at the 11th floor—the ship's control room, or the bridge as it was called on the ship. She guessed that Enrique had gone to see the Captain. What was Enrique up to?

She decided to go back to her room to call her friend Myra back home—a psychologist who always had good ideas for troubling events like the one Joanna had experienced. What would Myra suggest?

22

What Was It About Enrique?

Enrique went from spinning a surprise dance "tête-à-tête" with Ricky to dropping the whole idea of dancing altogether. He was so into Joanna's issue. Tina had to admit she was a little disappointed, even as she realized that Joanna was more important.

She'd feel better if she knew what Enrique was up to.

Enrique was laser-focused on Joanna. Tina thought encouraging Joanna to open up was the right thing to do—at least she hoped so. She didn't expect Enrique's intense response. After they talked, she wondered if he had something to do with the ship.

When she heard what happened, Sheila suggested that Tina keep Joanna away from the bars and away from some of the more lubricated guests. Enrique wasn't that type. That was certain from his reaction to Joanna's story.

Tina couldn't help but admire Enrique's "magic" with Joanna. Joanna calmed down after talking with Enrique. Why had he taken such an interest? What did he hope to accomplish? Was he interested in Joanna? She hoped not.

But so much about Enrique was a mystery. Tina assumed he was another passenger on the boat with the rest of the singles. Yet he seemed like more than that. He had such a way about him. He really seemed to know a lot about ships.

For his part Enrique knew exactly what he was doing and why he was doing it. His blood was boiling. He had a few things that he wasn't yet ready to share with Tina.

After Tina's phone call with her friend back home, she decided to be more proactive and learn more about Enrique. Tina wanted to ask her friend to google Enrique's name, but she needed a last name. She hoped Sheila would have additional information on Enrique.

Sheila had a hospitality office with a desk outside her door on the fifth deck aft section of the ship. She had asked for that office when it came available. It was next to the purser's office for the ship. His name was Carl Simmons, a third-generation Yale graduate who had convinced himself that he was the most important cog in the entire ship's wheel. Sheila took great pains to not dissuade Carl from that view. Carl was an important source of information, and he helped her fund her special event requests.

Carl and Sheila occasionally shared lunches. He liked her. She wasn't hard on the eyes. Carl was slim and trim with a handlebar moustache big enough for a pair of monkeys to swing on. Sheila wondered if those bars did the same nothing for other women as they did for her.

Carl also liked learning about the inside track from Sheila. He wanted to know what she knew. Sheila used those lunches to apply a little gentle pressure to advance special causes in which she had interest, things like getting new cutlery for Marietta and an occasional additional allotment for exotic foods for Georgio and Marietta.

If the handlebars weren't enough, Carl's other problem was that he talked incessantly. You couldn't shut him up. And he had an annoying habit of hanging on to the last syllable of words adding undue importance to the word.

"You know Sheila, Yale graduated more lawyers than any college in the entire United Staaaates!"

"Really," Sheila retorted. "How interesting." Of course it wasn't interesting at all, but Sheila played the game and he was part of her network.

Sheila was careful to not dissuade him from his grandiose thoughts. It seemed to keep his spirits alive—given that he had the most boring job ever: pushing numbers across a spreadsheet and saying "no" when he shouldn't always have to say no. Sheila worked hard to get all the "Yeses" that were available. It was in her DNA. She recognized that DNA in Tina too.

Between his self-important attitude and close talking, Sheila was pretty sure that poor Carl would be single for quite a long time. It was a shame. Carl wasn't a bad guy—just not very self–aware. She wondered if she could tell him without hurting his feelings. She hoped to pick just the right moment in one of their conversations to coach him to a better place.

When Tina arrived, Sheila was on the phone pushing housekeeping for better tablecloths for the dance.

"Come on Julio. You know those old grey linen tablecloths are hideous. They look like crap. We used the same ones last year. Break out the new heart-shaped ones I ordered. I saw the box when I went by your office this morning."

She listened for just a minute more before firing back, "Really, Julio. You think I give a damn about your budget?" She knew him well enough to push back hard.

She went on to tease him further, mimicking her own sicky-sweet southern belle voice as she pretended to talk to the Captain, "Oh, Captain, remember that party we had last year and Mrs. Alverna found her new husband, Rafe? That's the same party I'm planning this week. And Julio is using those same old ratty, raggy, tattered tablecloths. Can you help?"

As they bantered back and forth, Julio had an idea. He decided to ask Sheila first about his vacation—not the Captain, but Sheila. Sometimes the straightest way through is the fastest way. Sometimes the best way through something is to go around.

Julio had watched Sheila get her way long enough that he knew she could help him. He hoped to grab some time in Ajaccio, Corsica, in France. That was his real prize. He thought to himself, *the hell with the budget and those crappy old tablecloths. Here I come, sunny beaches and beautiful blue waters in Ajaccio right on the Mediterranean!*

"Okay, Sheila, we'll put out the new tablecloths tonight, but you owe me. When we get to Corsica, I need time off there. Can you back me up on that?"

"Oh, darlin,' why of course I can help." The words dripped out of her mouth.

With her on his side, Julio was pretty sure he was getting that time off.

Sheila hung up the phone very pleased with herself. Still enjoying her win, Sheila looked over at Tina.

"Hi Sheila," Tina said. "How's it going? I love, love, love the decorations for the dance."

"Do you really?" responded Sheila. "I spent two hours last night stringing those balloons. Not everyone likes them the way we romantics do. And the staff was too busy to help—so they said. But I love the feeling the balloons give. I love the ambiance. In my head I could see people kissing under the balloons as soon as I put them up."

She stopped and smiled at Tina. "You didn't come here to talk about decorations. What can I do for you?"

"Well, do you remember the little speech you gave at the beginning of the cruise? I was right in front listening. To be honest I grimaced when you said you were going to make sure we would all have the opportunity to fall in love. I even said to myself—that's a lie. So now, just days later, I think I'm here to eat a little crow – but I'm not sure."

Sheila loved the direction the conversation was headed. She looked at Tina, scrunched her nose and said in a drawly, Southern way, "Okay sweetiepie, tell me more."

Tina recounted to Sheila the whole trip-and-fall story about Enrique. Then she told Sheila about Joanna's misadventure with Ken. Sheila already knew but she didn't let on. Marietta had heard too. She remembered what Marietta said when she heard: "Dirty dishwater—that one!" It was Marietta's devil curse. The slinger was about to be slung but he didn't know it yet. He'd only been on the boat for six months and had done nothing but cause trouble. Sheila wanted to hear the details from Tina before she spoke.

After Tina recounted what she knew about the awful treatment Ken had given to Joanna, it confirmed what Sheila knew of the encounter.

Tina had been sidelined by the turn of the conversation with Sheila. What she really wanted to know about was Enrique. What did Sheila know about him? Was he a for-real single guy? What was his last name? Could he possibly be worth breaking the sugar-daddy taboo like her grandmother told her to do?

Sheila held her tongue about Enrique mostly. Yes, she thought he was nice. She didn't know a lot about the older gentleman. She knew he was important. He had the Captain's ear. Sheila had made her way on the cruise ship by paying attention to who knew whom. She was smart enough not to pry. She figured things out with her own little detective game of connect-the-dots. She looked for results. Who talked to whom, and what happened next?

She had seen Enrique speak to the head chef and the very next day, a new menu item appeared. It was a vegetarian dish "Baked Avocado Eggs" that she hadn't seen on the ship before. It was a piece of information she logged into her mainframe. Two and two was usually four, and sometimes five. She always got an extra kick out of knowing more than her shipmates did.

Tina pushed a smidge more. "You are the romance director," she said with emphasis as she batted her eyelashes. "What do you think?"

"Don't bat your eyelashes at me," Sheila sparked at Tina in pretend outrage.

"Whatever do you mean daaarling?" responded Tina as the two women playfully teased each other. "I mean, who are we talking about hooking up here?"

Tina blurted it out. "Me." She smiled.

"Well, there is the age difference," Sheila candidly observed. Tina smirked. Yeah, she knew that.

"Is he available or not?" Tina pushed sternly for an answer.

"I'm not sure." Arggh. Tina's stomach growled. Delay. Delay. Delay.

Sheila decided to encourage Tina. She was never sure about how these things would go. Despite her own experience, she felt that no one would ever find love if Cupid didn't at least point his or her arrow. Targets didn't have to be the same age, or the same type— whatever that means—or the same sex for that matter. Sheila had seen people of all stripes fall in love.

Sheila winked and said, "I'll look into a bit. See me after the dance. I promise I'll spill."

23

Enrique's Secret Past

Try as she might, Sheila was dead-ended in her inquiries about Enrique. Where did he come from? None of her many friends on board could tell her much about him. Marietta held her index finger and "shushed her" when she asked about Enrique. Sheila could tell that Marietta knew more but she didn't want to cross Marietta. "Shush" meant more than quiet. It was a warning to leave the subject alone, or else.

"Shush" frustrated Sheila. Nobody else seemed to know. She wondered how this mysterious gentleman with the light brown fedora hat integrated seamlessly and quietly amid the staff and upper management. Was he a modern-day James Bond with some strange mission on board the "Joys of Love"? She laughed to her-self. *Ridiculous!*

Carl was her "go-to" information guru. On the "QT" he looked Enrique up for her in the ship's manifest. He didn't have much. He offered a few details to fill in the puzzle. Just enough to keep

Sheila on his side, but not enough for her to thread the needle into Enrique's cover act of a gentleman traveler.

Enrique pre-paid his bill about three months before the cruise. He boarded in Miami with a large group that boarded from that city each year. Enrique stayed in a Class A balcony luxury suite overlooking the infinity pool and sculpture garden. Nice! Sheila knew guests paid handsomely for those suites.

"Carl, what's Enrique's last name?"

With a mini scowl, Carl responded, "He's on the Prima-1 list. You know what that means." His voice trailed off. Sheila did know. That was the ship's special incognito travel list for celebrities and guests who preferred to travel without being known. "I can lose my job for sharing that information," Carl added. "Not happening."

A celebrity, Sheila thought to herself. *Is he a movie star, or a big sports figure? Maybe he owns a soccer team.* Their itinerary intersected multiple large soccer venues.

She winced as she tried to calm herself down.

Interesting. Hmm. Alright then. She thought she'd try again. "Just give me an initial," she said.

Carl tersely fired back, "A, but not another letter!" *Wow*, Sheila thought, giggling to herself. *Maybe he is a foreign movie star.*

Sheila was pretty good at making conversation. She decided to get some answers face-to-face from Enrique. It was part of her job, she justified. How else could she find a good match for Enrique?

She checked out the lounge near the sculpture garden opposite Enrique's room. She'd have a coffee and chat up the guests until she found Enrique. When he arrived, she thought about teasing him with her inside information about Tina. She wouldn't spill all the beans, but enough to get Enrique talking. It was a grand plan—or so she thought.

Sheila waited in the garden for about an hour. She spotted Enrique leaving his room and heading toward her through the sculpture garden. She excused herself from a guest with whom she was chatting and wandered over to intercept Enrique.

"Hello, Enrique. How are you today? Are you enjoying the activities on board the 'Joys of Love.'"

Enrique was happy to see Sheila and greeted her warmly. He knew she was smart. She had a chance to prove it when they met the first time.

"Hi Sheila, I'm having a great time. After all, you are the 'love doctor' here, right?" he said teasingly with a big smile.

Gosh, he's smooth, Sheila thought to herself.

"Do you have a minute? I'd love to share some additional activities I've planned. Maybe you can join us."

Enrique looked at his watch. He had ten minutes to spare before his board meeting.

"Why I'd love to hear about your plans," Enrique said, as he pulled up a chair at a table near one of the beautiful green, animal-shaped plant sculptures. He invited her to sit with him.

He waited as she sized him up. He did the same with her. He looked over her big round sunglasses with yellow spots that matched her top. She wore a skort that exposed her tanned legs, and a gold ankle chain with a tiny heart. Enrique wondered who had given her the heart.

Sheila observed his brown-ribboned, tan fedora hat tilted to shade his brown eyes. His eyes leapt over her like a deer prancing over bushes into the woods to hide. He seemed to do everything fast, then settle back to slow. Weird.

"Well," Sheila continued, "we have a masquerade party on the top deck at 1900 hours and we're serving oysters and mushroom calamari. I've talked to a bunch of the pretty women on board and they're hoping some of the more handsome men like you will attend."

Sheila knew she was laying it on a little thick and stared at him for his reaction. Enrique didn't seem to mind. Enrique enjoined her with a question about Tina.

"Do you know if the young lady and her friend Joanna will be at the party?"

Perfect, Sheila thought. She almost gave him the direct answer, which of course she knew, but decided instead to play a bit of cat and mouse. Sheila really enjoyed these types of interactions. She was delighted when people squirmed with her strategic indirect nosiness.

"Which lady do you mean?" she said coyly.

"I think there was a lady with a black, string bikini at the pool, and I know another woman from Canada with two little dogs."

Sheila was in heaven playing her game with Enrique.

"Which young lady was it again?" she asked, watching the expression on his face. Her women's intuition sensed Enrique was sweet on Tina—she just didn't know how sweet. She was drawing her Cupid's bow and waiting.

Enrique took the light-hearted challenge and responded, "Oh, yes, I think it was the young lady with the black suit. I didn't notice that it was a string bikini," he responded equally coy with a big grin. He knew exactly to whom he was referring, but he was willing to play Sheila's game..

Sheila laughed and thought, *Gotcha!* "Yes, that's Tina. She'll be there. I think she likes you too!"

Enrique's pleased surprise showed in a lightning-quick smile. He covered it just as quickly and looked at his watch. She observed to herself, *More of that fast-then-slow stuff.*

"May I ask you where you are from, Enrique?"

"I'm from Italy. But I live mostly abroad," he replied.

Sheila sensed she was pushing a bit too hard and might work her way out of Enrique's good graces. She eased off.

Enrique took the hint and the lead and said, "It was very nice chat with you, Sheila. I'll definitely be at the next masquerade party. What should I wear?"

Sheila thought for a moment and said, "I'll have a perfect outfit ready for you. Meet me at the dance floor at 1830 hours."

Sheila was genuinely excited. With a big smile, she added, "I have a whole room full of colorful, dazzling costumes. I just need a body to put in them to excite our women guests. I'll size you into an outfit that will make the ladies swoon."

Enrique grinned with a shy wince, and in quiet excitement, emitted a gasp of incoming breath. For the first time in a long time—since his wife passed—Enrique felt a warm, tingling feeling. Was it in his chest? He thought about it. In that brief moment Enrique let go of his tight mental control of his animal instincts as his mind wandered lustfully to male-energized images of Tina at the pool. Discomfort grew in his mid-section. It wasn't his chest.

The visions of Tina and her tight, string bikini caught him by surprise. He cleared his throat.

He got up quickly, smiled at Sheila, and said, "I'll be there!"

He shook himself with a shiver from the top down as he walked away. *What a strange feeling*, he thought.

Sheila hadn't got much information out of Enrique, but there was plenty in their exchange to encourage Tina. She found herself tingling in anticipation of the party. She couldn't wait to see Tina.

Sheila had another meeting at the party area before she headed for her regular meeting with Marietta. On her way up the stairs she bumped into Tina.

Impatiently and excitedly, Tina asked, "Well, did you find anything out?"

"Not much," replied Sheila avoiding eye contact for a moment before she coyly broke into a broad smile and whispered, "But I did find out he's from Italy."

"What? Italy! Really." Tina gasped loudly. "I always wanted to go to Italy." *This is so cool*, Tina thought. She wanted to pinch herself. She had to slow down her racing thoughts.

The conversation also reminded Tina that she had to call the managing editor for her new travel article when she got back to her room.

Sheila got back to the business at hand and said, "Would you like me to help you pick out your masquerade party outfit for tonight. I could use your help to pick out a few different costumes for some of our other guests too. You have good taste in clothes. It might be fun."

Tina was excited to help and said, "Great! I'll meet you at the party deck in two hours." She needed the time to get organized and call the editor of "Travel the World In Style."

Back in her room she dialed up Roberto—the editor. Luckily, she got through quickly on the ship's Wi-Fi. "Roberto, do you remember me? It's Tina James. I wrote that article a few months back about single traveling."

"Of course, I remember you, Tina." Roberto responded, "We've gotten lots of good feedback on that article. It was so upbeat. Singles are a big segment of our market."

Roberto asked, "How can I help?"

Tina eagerly responded, "I've got an idea for another article."

"Okay. What's your idea?" asked Roberto.

"Well, I'm on a cruise ship now and I've been keeping a journal. It details how the crew and guests interact. There's lots of intrigue, a few bad characters, and great food. Honestly, the words are jumping from my brain onto the pages as I write.

"What do you think? Is it something you might publish?"

"Yes," Roberto responded without hesitation. "We've got sponsors that love your target market. In fact, my dad's on a cruise now. He embarked out of Miami."

"Really? It isn't the 'Joys of Love,' is it?" asked Tina.

"I'm not sure, but I think that might be the one he's on," replied Roberto.

"What's his name?" Tina asked.

"Enrique."

Tina just about jumped out of her skin. "Is he about fifty-five years old—maybe 5-9'?"

"Yeah, could be him. He looks younger but that sounds about right."

Tina thought about how crazy this trip was getting. First there was Ricky, the engineer from Ecuador, then the awful stuff with Joanna, and now Enrique was related to her editor. *Wow!* she thought.

"Oh my gosh! Really?" she gasped to Roberto, as she scrunched her face into a wide-lipped grimace and shivered. She couldn't believe her ears.

"Enrique's your dad?"

"Wait a minute," Roberto said with a kind-toned pushback. He was taken aback by this new turn of events and needed to slow Tina down. "It's probably best that you don't let on that you know. I'll tell you why later. Let's keep it a secret between you and me. Okay?"

Tina thoughts tumbled as she processed the information. *Is he married? Doesn't he talk to his kids? Could he be some kind of a recluse? Would she aggravate him if she asked his age? His status? Was he gay?* Tina's mind ricocheted back and forth with these questions and more kept coming. *What did he have to do with "Travel the World" magazine?* Tina's curiosity was through the roof. But she was worried too. Tina's fledgling, travel-writing career could be on the line. Her mind raced and spun like a pinwheel in a fast wind out on the deck of their ship.

Tina's thoughts came back to Sheila. She was in a bit of a "sticky wicket" as Granny used to say. *I feel awful. How can I keep this from Sheila? It would be dreadful especially after Sheila has been so nice.*

Oh, what a conundrum. Roberto insisted it be kept a secret. She wasn't going to screw up her chances.

Tina pulled herself back. She vowed that she wouldn't divulge a word of this. Still, she couldn't help but laugh to herself, as she checked her watch. It was 1400 hours ship time. How lucky she was to be able to get another article—on top of everything else. With all these rushing thoughts, she had to pinch herself to get back.

Roberto, who had been waiting for her trance to dissipate, finally pushed Tina for her response and asked again with concern in his voice, "Tina?"

"Yes, yes. Of course. Of course. A secret." Tina responded, "For sure I'll keep it a secret. I ran into your dad at one of the singles dances on board. He was very considerate to a friend of mine."

She found herself mumbling and cut herself short, "We'll talk later. Okay, Roberto?"

"I'm glad to hear of his kindness. That's definitely him."

Roberto replied with piqued interest. "You'll have to tell me more when we chat again. I look forward to your article."

"Ciao. Yes. Later," Tina responded.

She tried to calm herself. *Breathe,* she thought.

Breathe, Breathe, Breathe, she streamed into her own head.

Tina's creative energies and impulses were bubbling out of her, barely held back like horses gated before a race. She went to her room and as soon as she got there, she grabbed her notebook and started scribbling furiously. Thoughts of romance—her *own* romance—made her giddy.

Tina was even more excited than before. But now she had to keep the news about Enrique a secret. She thought about all the help Sheila had given her. "Eechh!" This would be a tough secret to keep. She wanted so much to share with her new friend.

But would she? Anyone trying to keep a secret would agree. This was a tough ask.

24

I Can't Wait to Tell You

As much as Tina wanted to know so much more about Enrique, she didn't want to betray Roberto's trust. That wouldn't help her career to go against her editor's wishes, never mind what other havoc it would wreak between herself and Sheila.

What was Enrique's role on the ship? Why was he on board? And why was he in contact with the Captain? So many questions. Why didn't anyone know about him. Her sleuth muscles were flexing behind the scenes.

It was crazy that Enrique was Roberto's dad. She felt she had to tell someone. She dialed up her mom after breakfast the next morning.

"Mom, you won't believe this. You know that older guy, the guy who stumbled into me on the deck and then bought me perfume?"

Her mom was incredulous. "No. T-T Sweetie, you definitely didn't tell me about an older guy buying you perfume. I would remember that." T-T was her mom's pet name for Tina.

Tina grimaced. She left that part out when she told her mom about Mr. Stumble and Bump.

She thought quickly, "Mom, I meant to tell you but so much happened this week. Remember the thing with Joanna?"

"Alright T-T," said her mom, a bit put off by her daughter's tactics. "Go ahead then—tell me about it now."

"Let's hear about this older gentleman. He is a gentleman, isn't he?" Tina's mom waited patiently for what she was sure was going to be a doozy of a made-up story, a whopper just like the ones she heard straight from the stills in the Virgina mountains. Tina's mom knew how to spin a yarn herself, and she sniffed this one coming like a hunting beagle after the shot. Moms aren't stupid. Like most moms, Tina's mom knew how to play the part to get more info. She knew tricks her daughter didn't know yet.

"T-T, what does this—ah, gentleman do for work?" Tina's mom waited. "He's probably younger than me, right?"

Tina's mom's cunning wasn't lost on her daughter.

Tina didn't know what Enrique did for work. She didn't know his age either, but she knew her mom wouldn't like it, even if Granny would.

She could hear Granny's voice in her head, "You just go on a find a rich one, now ya' hear. Never mind that sicky-sweet, lover's kissy-face stuff. You get a rich one. Cash in and play that guy and his wallet like a fiddle, you hear me now, T-T?"

Gosh, Tina missed her kick-ass, funny Granny. "I tells it like it is, and like it should be." She remembered Granny cackling like a hen because she was so full of her fun self.

"T-T," her mom pushed again, breaking Tina's drifting, wonderful reminiscing about her Granny.

"What was his last name again?"

Tina knew her mom was on the computer. *Ugh*, she thought to herself. She didn't know. It felt like she was right back in high school being grilled by her mom just before a date.

Tina didn't have much more to offer. That wasn't a good thing. After all, she and Enrique only had a few conversations after their chance bump-and-run meet-up. There was nothing more to share.

Or was there?

"Well ah, Ma. I think he's uh . . . an investor?" Tina furrowed her brow to buy time. "And his son is an editor of that magazine that published my article. I think he's legitimate."

"Le-gi-ti-mate." Her mom repeated the word slowly, pacing her slow, agonizing-to-Tina faux drama, as if slowing down to sip a too-hot soup.

"Really?" said Tina's mom. Legitimate, hmm. Well, that's a first for a description of a gentleman, isn't it?"

Tina thought to herself, *Ohhh, Shoot! Where is this going?*

Tina knew. Tina's mom could feel her daughter squirming right through the phone.

"T-T," her mom quietly spoke, "Should I be worried?"

"About what, Ma?"

Tina could feel her throat tighten. Her eyes closed and she could feel a shiver go through her shoulders as she thought about what to say.

"Jesus, Ma . . . really? Your imagination has really gotten the better of you. I gotta go. I'll call you tomorrow."

Tina hung up the phone quickly. Her mother wasn't done, but Tina was. They both had trouble sleeping that night.

Tina woke up to a ringing phone and an excited voice.

25

It's Hard to Get Home from Italy Without a Paycheck

The on-board speakers bellowed to the crew area below deck. "Second mate Ken to the Bursar's office pronto. Bring your gear."

The Bursar shouted loudly again into the speaker, "Bring your gear!"

Tina reached across the bed to the phone ringing in her ear, "Hello. Who is this?"

"Hi, Tina, it's Enrique. I hope I didn't wake you." Enrique cringed as he spoke.

"No, No." She lied, as she tried to pull herself together quickly. "Yeah, Enrique, well this is a pleasant surprise." *How did he get my number?* she thought as she jumped out of bed and ran to the closet.

"Oh, sorry for the short notice," Enrique said. "There is an important event up on the B deck overlooking the boarding ramp. I'm absolutely sure you'll be interested. Can you come up?"

"Ah, just a second," said Tina as she gathered her wits. "Sure. Sure. Give me ten minutes. Does that work?"

Enrique looked at his watch and responded, 'Yeah—but not much longer than that."

"Okay, I'll see you there." Tina responded, as she hung up the phone and scrambled for her clothes. What did Enrique want? And her next thought was, *What should I wear? Jesus, this cruise gets crazier every day.*

Tina chose a tight-fitting, bright green jumper that revealed a hint of cleavage. She wanted to look her best. It was partly her Type-A personality and, she had to admit, partly that she was attracted to and intrigued by Enrique. She pushed a brush through her hair, grabbed her lipstick, and raced out of her room and up to the B-deck to find out what was going on.

As she came out onto the deck, the morning sun was shining brightly. White cumulus clouds spotted the sky far above the horizon. She looked for Enrique and spotted his tan fedora in a group of people. Enrique saw her and waved to her from a perch at the rail overlooking the gangplank.

"Come on up," Enrique shouted.

Tina headed his way and caught sight of the mountains above the Campania Valley in the high mountains of Italy.

Gorgeous! Shades of green and light blue shifted with the movement of the clouds over the mountains. The Campania mountain slopes pulled her eyes along curtains of wavy green trees down to the blue waters on the shore, and then up back up toward the gangplank. It was a beautiful scene: mighty mountains, magnificent sun, and their massive ship linked together in the moment. A backdrop . . . but to what?

This was their last stop before they disembarked from their cruise. Tina noticed Enrique with some of the crew chiefs, and she recognized the Captain in his bright, gold-braided sleeves. Raoul was there too with Marietta, Siv, and Sheila.

Strange, she thought. All of the top brass were there. She was dying to know why.

Enrique waved her over. She ran oveer and stood next to him, but he said nothing. His quiet disciplined control was intentional. She was strangely calm in his presence. It was a good feeling. It made her wonder about her place with him. Did she have a place?

She remembered Flora May's predictions of destiny. Her spine tingled so much that she quietly shook out a shiver of energy through her shoulders to calm herself.

The ship was leaving port. It was a somber moment unlike the usual aplomb and fanfare when they left the other ports. Sometimes the locals provided a band as a send-off. Not this time.

No band here. It was a bit of a mystery that Tina didn't yet understand. Over Enrique's shoulder she could see the dock below. She noticed the young deck officer Ken, Joanna's nemesis. His head was down, one suitcase in hand, as he walked down the gangplank alone toward the pier.

Gunslinger had slung his last shot on this cruise. Ken was the last to disembark in Italy. The ship's mates pulled the gangplank back as the ship slowly inched away from the dock. Deck mates yelled, "Is she clear?"

"What about the boom tie?"

"Pier is clear!"

Communication was loud and terse, as they pulled the giant six-inch, tie-off ropes from the rusty, staghorn bollards at the edge of the pier.

The engines reversed to pull the bow outward and then clunked loudly into forward gear. The huge propellers churned up brown foam as the ship began to change direction and pull away.

Gunslinger's unimpressive figure shrunk in their view, not a moment too soon. He was one of those people you hope to never see again. Karma was a bitch—especially for Ken! She hoped his soul would face a mirror.

Tina had never been a big revenge person, but she had to admit, seeing Ken disembark in distress and shame made her feel pretty good.

Enrique reached for her hand and squeezed it softly. Her heart jumped and pounded in her chest. Every part of her lit up at Enrique's touch.

"That young man has a tough road ahead. The icebergs run deep for people like him. He's not steered clear of the icebergs of life for some time now. Someday I hope to see if fate can re-set his course."

Tina's mind reeled as she bounced her own negative thoughts against the hope-filled, transcendent wishes Enrique expressed. She felt smaller.

Enrique looked into her eyes and asked, "Do you ever feel the need for a best friend?" He was looking through her and into her, piercing her shell, the outer piece everyone else got to see. She felt he was inside her.

"Yeah," she replied in a quiet whisper. The intensity of the question surprised her.

She took a deep breath and quietly exhaled air through her lips and downward onto her chin. Tina took a deep slow breath, tilted her head, gave Enrique an inviting smile, and said, "I've been looking for a long time for that."

They were headed out to the Mediterranean Sea, and back home. A slight sadness crept in as slowly as the ship departed the land. She hesitated. Was she also heading for an iceberg or was this budding relationship a piece of the sunshine she hoped would finally break through the clouds?

Tina exhaled again.

She looked over to Enrique and for the first time, she saw him in a different light. She admired him. He had touched her heart. His compassion and ability to view the situation with such detachment demanded her attention.

Enrique reached inside of her to demand she re-invent herself. She didn't want to. Joanna's situation was still raw. Finding understanding wasn't the plan. Her feelings surprised her.

Enrique's depth appeared in stark contrast to her first encounter with Mr. Stumble-and-Trip. Still, she was more puzzled than ever about what Enrique had to do with this "gangplank show"? Why was Enrique with the Captain and his leadership team?

She needed to know. The search engine inside her head was full steam ahead. She had to know more about this new "best friend" who was pushing her to be a better person. It was like having a set of keys but not knowing which locks they go in.

Frustrating!

Where could she find what she needed to know?

She re-traced what she knew. Enrique was Roberto's dad but Roberto had clammed up. Enrique seemed to know virtually everyone on board who had a position of power. And yet none of them were forthcoming about who Erique was, or what his role on board was.

Enrique seemed to have orchestrated the gangplank exhibition. As she sifted through the information, her reporter brain shifted to detective.

Bingo! It hit her. An idea sprung into her head. It would be easy enough to test. She'd go straight to the source.

She thought ahead as she rolled the question out in her mind, "Enrique—you got more explaining to do."

26

Turning the Screws

Tina flicked through her contacts to find Roberto's phone number. Roberto was the editor of "Travel the World in Style" magazine, but that wasn't why she needed his number. She had spoken to Roberto and found out Enrique was Roberto's dad. Roberto stopped short of giving anything else away. But now, no excuses. She needed to know.

Who was Enrique? What was his connection to the ship? What did Enrique have to do with the travel magazine business?

She had felt so close to Enrique when they spoke the day before. The connection they felt was obvious to each of them. Enrique knew it when he held her hand.

She thought he was not only affectionate but transparently decent in a way she had never seen or thought possible. She was amazed at how he framed the Gunslinger's mentality. Enrique had shown so much compassion, yet the consequences were strong. It was amazing to witness.

She got through to Roberto. "Roberto, this is Tina. Do you remember me?"

"Oh yeah," said Roberto, "I know who you are. My dad and I spoke several nights back. It seems you and he hit it off."

Tina's heart thumped in her chest. If she was near a mirror, she'd see her heart vibrating through her clothes in her reflection.

Roberto extended, "My dad feels that people who have not had a good start in life need a chance to prove themselves by being placed in hard situations to see if they deserve a second chance.

Roberto continued, "I understand you witnessed my dad's 'justice system' at work.

Tina replied, "I don't understand. Can you help me with all of this? What does Enrique have to do with the ship and this sailor who got removed from the ship?"

Tina was more puzzled than before.

Roberto began to fill the gap. "I think Dad's going to fill you in himself when you see him."

Roberto approved of Tina. She was spirited as hell. He let Enrique know he had Roberto's blessings. Anything more would have to come from Enrique.

He pivoted their conversation by saying, "I look forward to reading more articles. I'm sure we'll chat again. You'll be hearing from my dad soon."

"Caio."

"Roberto?" Click. The call ended.

It was maddening to Tina. What wasn't Roberto telling her? She was determined to get to the bottom of this mystery. Tina had

Enrique pegged as an Italian movie star or polo player. But what if he was a crime boss—mafia? She hoped not with all her heart.

Enrique would disappoint most of her guesses.

27

Discomfort on the Bridge

Enrique needed to find Tina. He hated not being direct with her. He didn't have time to make things right. It had been a busy day—too many damn meetings. He couldn't wait to find Tina, get away from all the "unnecessary" work, and get out to the ocean air. It was the best part of his job.

Like an experienced card player, Enrique had learned to keep his cards close. He kept his personal information wrapped tightly. His grandfather had always said, "Anonymity is a gift." Enrique took that to heart.

Yet sometimes he felt that he presented a mere shadow of himself, standing back behind the figure others saw. He wanted Tina to see past the shadow.

He stepped out from the bridge where he had met the Captain. Tina gazed out at the horizon near where they had met earlier.

Enrique had found many of his own answers gazing out to that very horizon.

Enrique skillfully climbed down from the bridge and approached Tina.

"Tina, how nice to see you," he added with a warm voice and a broad smile.

Tina was in deep thought.

Enrique observed Tina's quiet demeanor and the look on her face. Was it curiosity or confusion—or perhaps impatience? Her eyebrows were up—eyes askance—the right side of her mouth turned downward. He didn't know her well enough just yet, but he guessed she was sifting through all the little encounters in her life for connections, hoping for it all to make sense.

Horizons do that for you—like looking into a dancing fire on a cold night. Your thoughts touch each other with barely traceable, fine lines before jumping back to the unreachable places where they live in the back of your mind.

Hmm, Enrique mused, *what is she thinking?*

Shaking off her deeper thoughts, Tina began conversing with playful banter. "Ah, it's the mystery guy himself. So tell me, mystery guy, how does a person like you get to a place on a great ship like this overlooking the water?

"Well," Enrique started. "I guess it starts with loving the sea."

"Uh-huh," escaped Tina's lips. She caught herself and pursed her lips. The next move had to be Enriques's.

Enrique realized he had to be more forthcoming about his situation. "Well, I've always liked sailing and cruising," said Enrique.

Tina waited. She let the warm breeze fill the space between them.

"I work in the travel industry," Enrique confessed to a bare minimum story.

Tina gave a barely perceptible nod. She wasn't offering anything else until she knew more about her mysterious, hand-holding acquaintance.

Enrique reached for Tina's hand with his left hand and waved his right hand out toward the sea. "It's beautiful, isn't it?" he added.

He was drawn to the reflection of the sun in her eyes. Before he knew it, he reached to embrace her. He paused. He didn't say anything.

Tina wanted to pull away. Or did she? She wasn't sure. She couldn't escape his eyes. The two of them were like large magnets being pulled together by an invisible force. She couldn't move. She felt like she was in a trance.

"Tina?"

She felt like her tongue was trapped. It couldn't move. She was frozen to Enrique. Short breaths escaped quietly escaped her chest. For a brief moment he looked down into her tanned chest. As he shook his eyes back to her eyes, their noses brushed by one another, and their lips touched. Their first kiss wasn't a mistake kiss. They couldn't shy away from each other. She had never felt such magnetism.

Tina shivered as their lips locked. Her tongue tingled as it slid by Enrique's lips in mutual gentle affection. They were locked together, neither one wanting to break their embrace or shield themselves or their tongues from the moment.

Don't let this moment go, Tina shouted to herself.

Feeling the closeness, Enrique echoed similar thoughts. *Don't let her go. Hold on forever.* And he might have if the moment wasn't interrupted by panicked shouts.

"Man overboard!" shrieked the midsection deck hand.

No! No! No! This can't be happening, Enrique thought.

He jumped into action, shredding Tina from himself. He yelled to the deck hand, "Hit 7 Star on the comm panel. Tell them, engines to a slow stop."

Tina quickly shook herself into a surprisingly fast reaction.

Enrique raced toward the rear stairwell. Pointing to the far guard rail, Enrique shouted, "Grab that lifebuoy ring. I'll see if I can find the overboard."

Tina did exactly as Enrique demanded. She was amazed at how quickly he had jumped into action and down the stairs. She followed him.

"Over there," he pointed. "We need to get down to the lowest deck in the back. Give me the buoy."

With a practiced toss, he let the buoy fly like a frisbee into the wind. The rope trailed the spinning buoy as it landed just feet away from the struggling woman in the choppy blue water.

Enrique tied the rope end to the rail—leaving extra slack to allow for the swells in the ocean below.

Enrique estimated she had fallen some sixty feet into the water. He grabbed a nearby flotation vest, pointed at a comm pad near Tina and he yelled, "Hit Star 9 on that comm pad and call for lifeboat aft, lower deck. Emergency STAT. Got it?"

Tina nodded hesitantly and did exactly as she was told. In an instant, she screamed the message into the receiver: "Lifeboat aft lower deck, Emergency STAT!"

She got it right. Her heart was racing. Crew members arrived quickly and peered over the rails.

The responding officer in charge quickly called out on the intercom, "This is not a drill. One lifeboat to the water. Man overboard. STAT on aft deck three. Repeat, one lifeboat to the water on aft deck three."

Enrique leapt over the rail and jumped into the water. It was a thirty-foot drop from deck three. Enrique was a world-class swimmer. Tina didn't know that when he jumped. Her heart sank.

"No!" she yelled, but nothing loud enough to make a difference came out of her mouth. Her voice had no effect on the scene playing out before her. The next thing she saw was Enrique's body knifing through the surf below. She shivered as she counted while he plunged deeper and deeper—one, two, three, four, five, six, seven.

"Jesus," she gasped.

Suddenly, like a cork, Enrique popped up to the surface and started swimming toward the woman and the life buoy, uniting them both.

The crew on the deck around her was fast at work. Pulleys clanged, ropes flew, horns blared, emergency lights shrieked at her eyes. A winch lowered a lifeboat into the water with four crew members in less than two minutes. The crew steered to the woman and pulled her aboard. Enrique floated near the boat waiting for the crew to attend to the woman.

Tina wanted to know who her mystery man was. The scene before her was a road map of Enrique. He wasn't a regular, sports-loving, "meet in the street" guy. He was different—and special—that was certain. Only now she had more questions than before.

It took an hour to get the rescued woman, Enrique, the lifeboat, and the crew back on board. Enrique had to brief the Captain, and grab a change of clothes, before he could get back to Tina.

He hoped she understood.

Tina reminded him of his wife. Was she like his wife, or wasn't she?

You Got Some Splainin' To Do

Tina's friend Rita back home used a delightful expression at odd times such as this—like a car crash, or an unexpected break-up, to which she'd respond with her den-mother attitude and full curiosity mode, "You got some splainin' to do."

This incident needed serious explanation. It was traumatic, unforeseen, and amazing. It was beyond anything she'd ever witnessed first-hand.

While Tina waited for Enrique, she dialed up her mom to tell her about the rescue. Her mom was astounded. She wanted to know more about Enrique; Tina did too.

As soon as she could, Tina sent a note via the crew to Enrique to meet once he was finished with the rescue. Tina wanted the book on Enrique. She waited for Enrique in the upper bar away from all the rescue excitement.

As he approached, with a stern look on her face, she smirked at Enrique and said, "You definitely got some splainin' to do!"

Enrique smiled, then broke into a tension-relieving, extended laugh. It was the kind of laugh that comes up from your belly and makes your chest, the sides of your stomach, and your back hurt from the repetitive bellowing. He couldn't stop laughing.

Each time he looked at Tina and began to explain, he laughed again and again. He felt his cheeks and face fill with blood. His face flushed red. His grin got broader and broader. He thought his face would crack if his smile got any wider. Tina couldn't help herself either. She laughed so hard she thought she would pee herself.

After a few minutes of back and forth laughing, and guffaws, Enrique had to keep his head down to avoid her eyes and to avoid more laughter. He couldn't look in her eyes—those beautiful eyes—without losing it and cracking up.

"Get me a drink, will ya?" he squeaked out with half of his breath and half of his usual voice to the bartender. Enrique's hoarse voice was barely audible. He grunted and caught his breath before saying, "Not one of those girly drinks either—a Manhattan on the rocks."

They laughed hysterically at, and with one another in one of those inane moments that caused tears to roll onto their cheeks.

Tina tilted her head and sarcastically said. "Really? You, the great mystery-swimmer-sailor, can't have a girly drink?"

More laughter.

"Why is that?"

"Really?" he gasped between laughs.

Eventually they calmed down. Tina started her questions with the laser focus of a journalist; one who had to report to her mom.

Enrique stared at Tina for an uncomfortably long time. Tina waited. She refused to be intimidated. Instead, she looked Enrique in the eye and said, "Okay, so what was that rescue all about? It was a command performance that included a kamikaze dive to save that woman. It was truly amazing."

"I have so many questions now. I have to know," Tina continued. "Who in the hell are you? And why are you on this ship?"

Enrique cleared his throat and slowed himself down into the moment; something he had learned to do in dealing with tense issues over many years of business. He then repeated and answered Tina's questions one at a time. "What was the rescue about? It's simple. Someone needed help. I was there. I helped. That's all. I'd hope the same would be done for me," he said.

"Who am I? I'm Enrique Marianni."

He tongue-rolled the "r's" in Enrique, and Marianni, and emphasized with pride the last syllable in his first and last name.

Enrique playfully repeated his name, "Enrrrique Marrrianni."

"What in the hell am I? The jury is still out on that one," he said with a good-natured smile. "And why am I on this beautiful ship? I am an investor in the company that owns her. Add to that, like yourself, I needed a vacation."

Another broad smile.

"I hope that's enough for you. It's been a long day. The rest is a long story."

Tina rolled her eyes. Her mom's voice chirped in her head, *Oh no, you don't.* And before she could catch herself, Tina's Granny's expression just popped right out of her, "This onion is going to get peeled RIGHT NOW. I'm not buying the short story or waiting for the long one either. I want to know exactly what is really going on. All of it."

She surprised herself with her boldness.

"Fair enough," Enrique said, as he sat down next to her.

It was strange. Enrique normally didn't allow himself to be pinned down, but Tina had an unusual disarming effect on him.

Perhaps he was feeling the triple effect of Tina, Tina's mom, and Tina's grandmother rising through Tina.

Enrique thought back to the first time he saw Tina on the fifth-floor yoga deck when he stumbled as he got near her. She really did throw him off his game.

"Perhaps we should get a drink. I'm expecting a good explanation," insisted Tina.

Then in a charming, disarming little tease, she threw Enrique a head-tilt and a hair-throw as she winked at him. She knew full well that she was pinning him down with her "feminine" advantage too. He seemed nervous, especially for a guy who had just saved someone's life.

Enrique countered with his own spin after absorbing her little "family fastball."

"Do you mind if I smoke a cigar? We'll make it a celebration," Enrique asked.

"Be my guest." Tina played along.

She didn't like smoking, but if it helped Enrique explain this bizarre event, and who he really was, then she'd ride this one out.

She'd follow the swirls of the smoke wherever his cigar would take them.

Enrique stared at Tina's blue, tight-fitting outfit in anticipation of her next question. He felt a strange familiarity. What was it about Tina? Then it hit him. Tina reminded him of his wife. He heard a bee buzz in his ear. Was it real?

It had been a long time since Marilyn Marianni had passed. She was the love of his life. Whenever he met a woman, he would always compare her to his wife. Was she as smart as his dear Marilyn? Was she as gracious? Did she love people the way Marilyn did? Did she love children? His questions were unfair. No one could live up to her.

Enrique knew it was dangerous to compare women he met to his late wife. Still, he couldn't help but notice how Tina matched Marilyn's tenacity and poise. Tina engaged him with a spark for life he rarely experienced. It excited him.

Quite a few women had felt the sting of those comparisons without being told what had bitten them or what those comparisons were.

It could have been the reason that his relationships after Marilyn were doomed. It seemed every woman was an ill-positioned outsider and a threat to Enrique's memories. None could break through Enrique and Marilyn's shell.

Their shell poised at the ready with a stinging curse until now.

29

The Stinger: Enrique's Wife

Enrique and Marilyn met at a wedding in Italy when they were in their early twenties. Marilyn captivated Enrique from the first moment he laid eyes on her. Marilyn, on the other hand, had ideas that didn't include the young aspiring sailor sitting across the table from her at her uncle's wedding.

Marilyn danced and pirouetted throughout the evening staying away from the awkward young man Enrique certainly was. She had lots of suitors. Enrique sought every opportunity to be close to her. He offered her a drink only to be brushed away as if he was a fly on her food. It was unexpected treatment for the up-and-coming sea merchant.

She wore a stunning, bright-yellow, pleated dress with "have-to-look" cleavage that couldn't be avoided once a person came into her personal space. The dress fell delightfully on her shoulders. The pleated bottom lifted parachute-like in a way that captured every eye in the dance hall as she spun to every corner of the floor with multiple partners—except Enrique. For Enrique the story was simple—access denied.

Her dance card was full. The men approved of her impressive, good looks and elegant style. Not everyone in the halls was so appreciative. Jealousy shaded the eyes of many of the women in the hall.

Enrique didn't know how to catch her attention or even break into a short conversation, let alone how to gain her trust and begin his conquest. Enrique was smitten but "lost at sea." He felt like one of the gulls following the fishing boats for scraps.

It took most of the evening before he finally talked himself into asking her for a dance. Out from his lips popped a broken sentence, "M, mmm . . . mind dancing?"

Gracefully accepting his stumbled entreaty, she gave him a once over and thought to herself, *why not?*

He wasn't a good dancer, something she observed quickly. He wasn't a smooth conversationalist either. He was embarrassed and tongue-tied.

Whether it was out of pity or curiosity, Marilyn tried to set him at ease.

"Relax," she said. "Women practice dancing more than men. It's okay."

She liked Enrique right away for having the guts to ask her to do something he wasn't good at. It didn't stop Marilyn from teasing him mercilessly with her next question. "What else can't you do well?"

They knew instantly that they were a fit. Enrique loved the question and grinned. This was a woman Enrique wanted to know beyond her obvious good looks. He was a man that appreciated a challenge. She wouldn't disappoint him.

Marilyn smiled graciously and looked into the eyes of the handsome, nervous young man in front of her. She tried to remember every detail as she looked upon him. Her mom would want to know all about him and what she saw.

Enrique was staring at Tina, but Enrique's thoughts weren't about the woman in front of him. He had drifted back to his first meeting with Marilyn. The bee was ready, circling and buzzing before a sting.

Enrique drifted back and forth from Tina to Marilyn and their unique love. Her loss was like a straitjacket hindering his movement since her death. Marilyn wouldn't have wanted that.

For him, it didn't matter who his romantic interest was. Comparisons were inevitable. Tina was the latest victim—or perhaps he was the victim—trapped and chained to the past. It was a duel with himself. Was this another of life's cruel jokes?

"Enrique!" Tina snapped at him in a flirtatious way. "Where are you, mystery man?"

Enrique didn't say it, but Tina's little jab with her penetrating voice jolted him out of his melancholy memories. He decided to play along.

"Well, let's see. I'm on a boat at the upper bar with a beautiful woman named Tina."

He'd done it, or maybe Tina had. He felt his shoulders release tension.

It was the first time in years that he avoided the paralysis and sting of his past relationship and life. *How odd*, he thought. He didn't want to obscure the past. He thought of Marilyn every day. He had no interest in erasing those memories. Those memories were *their* memories. They cast big shadows. Those shadows rimmed the future with heavy lines. He couldn't decide if those lines contained the past or prevented the future. That dilemma would have to wait.

He pulled himself into the present and smiled at Tina. It both hurt and was a relief. Now he had to face the most difficult question of all: Would Marilyn forgive him?

30

Free to Fly

Wherever Marilyn was, she forgave him. Enrique was sure of it. The feeling rinsed over him like the gentle, soft swells of the ocean on a balmy, beach-day afternoon. He looked at Tina. They laughed for no reason. It was the easy laugh of two people who did that hard-to-do thing: live in the moment.

All of his tomorrows after Marilyn had been hard. He knew his life would be even harder if he was saddled with bad feelings about a new relationship. He wanted to be free to fly and cleansed from any guilt relating to Marilyn.

Tina had the same dilemma as Enrique—not only to be free of memories that prevented new relationships, but in her case the heartbreak stories that pricked her like a sewing needle whenever she thought about a new relationship. She wondered if she should share those stories with Enrique. Or was that simply baggage she should keep to herself?

Enrique wanted to share more about Marilyn with Tina. He wasn't sure whether to mention Marilyn or how much to share. Maybe sharing would provide the freedom he desperately sought.

Tina's thoughts mirrored Enrique's. She decided to reveal her feelings. She laid out her self-doubting corkscrew face and with a smile asked, "Do you mind sharing about your wife?" Tina hoped her candor would uncork their relationship. It did.

Enrique was pleasantly surprised. He took a puff on his cigar, as if to clear his thoughts. He released the smoke slowly and intentionally with an individual thought riding on each curl of smoke.

What should he say? How candid could he be? Would Tina be scared off if she knew how much his wife was part of him at every moment? He decided to take a chance.

"Well, thanks for asking," he began. "Marilyn was a ray of sunshine in everything she did, and everything I did. Honestly, I can't even begin to tell you the hole she left in my life."

He paused for a moment to collect his thoughts.

"Go on," said Tina.

"Once, when we were out to dinner, a young toddler walked away from his parents at the next table and came right to Marilyn. She had a magnetic attraction to children. Before you knew it, the little boy was on her lap and she was singing some little silly tune about a bunny."

Enrique's eyes became misty. Tina felt a sinking feeling as she observed Enrique's face.

Tina wondered how to restore the light in the room, in their presumed relationship, as fledgling as it was.

Enrique provided a flickering match as he continued his story.

"The little boy had become squeamish and looked for his parents. Marilyn handled endings so well. She tapped the little boy on his bottom and said, 'Free to fly little one. Free to fly.'"

"Then Marilyn pointed the little boy to his parents and off he ran to their waiting arms."

Enrique looked at Tina, "I feel like that right now. Free to fly."

Relief swept over Tina; Enrique had opened up to her.

31

Another Way Out

By some strange twist of fate, in a short amount of time—less than a week—Tina and Enrique had built a bridge together. But to where? Enrique's path to closure with Marilyn etched its way on their canvas.

Tina had her own devils too. Dead end relationships with men who didn't fit her vision of what she and someone else should look like. Tina had several romances that reached the "almost" stage. There were some swift, luck-less and nasty breakups too.

Her past choices had somehow always missed the mark. She knew Enrique was different. For one thing, he was older. His age was like a double-edged sword that split her thinking in two ways: Enrique was sharp, articulate, wise, and good looking. But was Enrique the one to salve her romantic impulses? Could she dare to think of him as her soulmate? She couldn't believe that thought even crossed her mind.

What would she say to all the naysayers?

To open up to Enrique meant danger and potential injury to her self-esteem, risk to the little girl inside her that she tried so hard to protect.

What would Granny say? That was an easy one. She pictured Granny with a devilish pitchfork prodding Tina from behind into Enrique's arms. No steps back without an OUCH! Keep moving—straight toward to the thing she feared—love and its partner . . . loss.

Tina could hear Granny speaking to her, "This one is different. He is a keeper."

How strange it was to listen to the inner voice of her Granny. Could Tina overrule her fear?

Tina looked into Enrique's eyes hoping to transfer some kind of telepathic truth. She asked, "Did you ever feel someone from your past was telling you what to do?"

Enrique softened his eyes, took a breath, and with obvious understanding said, "Oh, yeah. I've felt a voice in my head many times over the last twenty years."

This was Tina's chance. She felt close enough to Enrique to push for answers from his past. Ever since their chance meeting at yoga on the second day, and his flower-laced apology, she had felt he was different. Who was he really? She knew very little about him. Her inquiries were stymied. Mystery surrounded him.

The way he handled the man-overboard situation was amazing. Enrique piqued her interest in so many ways. She wanted to understand what made him tick.

She thought back to the episode with the dirtbag officer Ken and how Enrique handled that situation with class and more grace than she felt she could ever muster. Enrique hadn't been willing to permanently condemn Ken as she had. Enrique showed an unusual level of restraint regarding Ken's long-term outlook. Enrique had left room for hope and change. Tina hoped to explore that scenario when the two of them had time. She sensed that Enrique had wisdom and understanding she didn't possess. She knew she could learn from him.

Enrique said, "People like Ken, like all of us, are not naturally bad. Human nature is a beast within all of us that needs to be tamed."

Tina was struck by his words; the wisdom she heard. She could feel Enrique's wisdom seep into her, not in a gentle way, but not abruptly either. His thoughts crept into her consciousness the way cold creeps into your body on a dark, still, icy winter night when you sleep—slowly, drifting between the pillow and your head— relentlessly. She felt herself fighting those thoughts, trying to put layers on her thoughts to protect herself. His words were numbing in a way she couldn't identify; darker, deeper, more penetrating, almost as if his words snuck into her and attached themselves to her.

Tina's thoughts jumped rapidly from introspection to his words as they cut a path into her soul. She pulled herself back. She realized she needed more questions answered.

"Enrique, how is it you know the Captain again?"

Enrique squirmed. It was time. Enrique needed to unburden himself.

He still had doubts. Who could blame him? In his position it was important to know. Enrique needed to know Tina's heart. More pragmatically, he needed to be sure Tina wasn't a gold digger.

"Tina, if you had all the money and means to change your life, what would your life become?" he asked. "How different would it be?"

She thought about asking him the same question. Instead, Tina replied, "Honestly, I've never let money control my life. Money doesn't drive me or my decisions. I wouldn't be here right now if money drove me. I've been searching for my best path for a long time—searching for me. I haven't felt clarity for my purpose or place in life. Do you know what I mean?"

Enrique did know what she meant. He felt self-doubt too—especially at this moment.

She added, "I can't imagine that I would change. I've had a few chances at that pot of gold. I didn't take the bait. I'm a sucker for true love." She winced internally and wondered if she had shared too much. Perhaps she had been too direct.

Tina thought back several years to a marriage offer she had refused from a wealthy oil man. She second guessed herself for years afterward. Her Granny was pissed about that guy.

That cowboy always wore a wide-brimmed hat that made his head seem even bigger than it was. Dobbs—Jason Dobbs. That was his name. She knew she wasn't a money grabber. Dobbs was her chance to grab the pot of gold. He was a nice enough guy, but she couldn't do it. They weren't perfect for each other. It had to be perfect. They didn't have the connection she needed.

Tina's thoughts drifted off to her "perfect-fit" person. Her dream guy had to be compassionate and smart—a thinker. She had turned down Jason Dobbs. She also turned down her fill of dumbasses, and even some nice guys. She had made more than her share of relationship mistakes. She suffered her mom's scornful eyes for many of those misses.

Now older, Tina wanted a relationship with a principled man who knew himself. She had grown tired long ago of the stuck-in-adolescence, sports goons whose bravado overcame their decency seemingly at every opportunity. Tina's match had to be serious, but he also had to know to live in the moment; someone who understood how fleeting life could be; how precious each drop of sunlight and darkness was. Her match had to be a person with depth and caring; someone who had a few miles and the wisdom that came with those miles.

It was a tall order. Was Enrique capable of that? What would her friends say? He was older than her by a generation, her parents' generation. That part didn't matter to her. Tina had left most of her friends and their opinions behind when she made up her mind to leave her steady insurance job and reach for the stars to become a travel writer. Most of those friends were tied to their upbringing. They were "homeys" tied to the cards they were dealt. Tina's best friends would have a lot to say either way.

Tina struggled to stay focused. Her thoughts ping-ponged between Enrique directly in front of her and her sense-making of whatever this "involvement" was.

If Enrique and Tina got together, her not-really friends (we all have those) would take a few jealousy-based swings on social media and in private gossip sessions. She could live with that.

Tina was different. She had cut the umbilical cord. She was trying hard to find herself. If Enrique was to be in her path, she needed more from Enrique. She needed to be convinced.

She had tried to figure out Enrique. His handling of the officer who had hurt Joanna was part of the puzzle. She decided to ask Enrique. "Do you remember that dirtbag officer Ken who hurt my friend?"

Enrique acknowledged with a nod.

Tina continued, "Even though Ken was a dirtbag, you chose a muted response, wisdom over harshness. Your attitude was one of compassion. I have to know. How do you get to that place of compassion? I haven't been able to get there."

"Ah," Enrique said. "That." He rubbed his chin, let out a sigh, and pressed a frown on his face.

"I think it comes from people lots smarter than me. I read a lot. Rumi, the Persian poet said, 'Somewhere out there, beyond right and wrong, there is a field. I will meet you there.' In my quiet times, that sentiment strikes me as I try to take on its depth. I lean on that kind of wisdom when problems arise."

Tina shook her head to clear her thoughts. That was deep. It felt good to hear it from a person she felt close to.

Tina asked, "Do you remember when I spoke to Roberto about the article I wrote? I asked him about you. He said that you would tell me yourself when the time was right. So I'm asking, who are you, really?"

After a long pause, Enrique's cigar found its way to his lips. He blew out a circle of smoke. The smoke hovered in the nighttime air, as if the fleeting smoke itself held the key to his secrets. "As I was saying, my family invests in the travel business."

Before he could finish his thought, Siv, the yoga instructor, happened by. "I haven't seen either of you at yoga. Will you be coming for our afternoon session?"

Siv noticed the two of them seemed close.

"We aren't sure," said Enrique with a querying look toward Tina.

Tina thought it sounded odd that Enrique had referred to the two of them as "we," a combined unit, so to speak. She liked the thought. It was a milestone. It was nice.

"Yes," she added with a smile. "If Enrique can spare the time. We'll be there."

Enrique noticed Tina had spoken for him. It pleased him. He didn't quite know why.

Then Siv turned directly to Enrique. "Mr. Arnoldo, could I have a moment. It's about the yoga space."

Enrique looked slightly embarrassed, but he nodded. Tina had seen the Arnoldo name but couldn't remember exactly where saw it. Then it hit her. It was on the brochures in her room. She tried not to let her surprise show.

She wouldn't forget his name. Siv seemed to be the only one on board who knew it. Enrique Arnoldo. She hoped her mystery man had good news behind the curtain. She couldn't wait to get to her phone and her computer. She could only imagine what she'd find out. She wondered if that was why Enrique knew the Captain.

32

Enrique Arnoldo's Captain Connection

As Siv left them, Enrique turned to Tina and said, "Let's take a walk and get some fresh air."

They moved toward the upper deck. Enrique explained, "Our family runs a travel business with lots of pieces. What would you think if I told you that my responsibilities include watching after this ship. That's how I know the Captain."

"Well," Tina responded. "That seems like a big responsibility."

"Yeah," Enrique responded thoughtfully. "There is a lot to it—a lot of square pegs and round holes."

Tina wasn't sure what Enrique meant, but she was ready to listen.

Enrique continued. "Things go wrong all the time. I think it is the nature of things—to go wrong, not right. Catching those wrongs before things turn ugly is the trick."

Tina's mind was cranking out thoughts and lots of questions as fast as she could. "So is that why you were ready when the woman went overboard?"

"Yeah, I suppose," said Enrique. "Years of watching over things keeps you alert and ready most of the time. Although I still miss things that I shouldn't."

Enrique continued, "I've eaten some well-deserved humble pie over the years. This work certainly keeps a person's ego in check." Tina loved what she was hearing. "I don't need to be taking any victory laps. That's for sure. Earlier you mentioned our friend, the junior officer Ken?"

Tina nodded. Of course, she remembered that dirtbag.

"Well, I approved his hire. I'm smack in the middle of that mess too," Enrique said.

Tina was incredulous. "You oversee hiring?" she asked. There was a lot more to Enrique than she could have guessed.

"Well, no. Not really," said Enrique. "But I oversee management. I guess I'm chief cook and bottle washer here, too."

Tina opined, "Sounds like there is a lot on your plate. No pun intended."

Enrique laughed. As they approached the bow, the moon lit their path. Mist covered the stairs. Enrique wanted to abandon all thoughts of his ship business. It was play time—or at least get-away-from-work time—or so he thought.

He reached for Tina and slid his hand into her hand. Quickly pointing to the stairs, he guided them up. A full moon greeted them at the top of the landing and stopped them in their tracks. Tina's hair danced in the ocean air. Enrique pulled Tina close to him, tenderly bracing against her and the circular steel rail as the ship rocked gently side-to-side through the ocean swells. She felt the hard rail press against her as they embraced.

Their eyes locked. Another kiss? His mind raced. She was a jumble of emotions ranging from fear to excitement.

Enrique slowed himself. Too many eyes. He looked around. It was safe enough. He pulled her close. Her heart pounded.

As he leaned toward her, head tilted down, her lips brushed softly and tenderly across his. Tina's upper lip slipped between Enrique's lips. The delicate touch of his tongue moistened her lower lip. She gasped for a breath and pulled away. The suddenness surprised her. He pulled her back. She fled back into his strong embrace. She wanted to bite his lip ever so gently, but was interrupted when Enrique's phone chimed. He sighed and looked down at his phone.

"Sorry." He clenched his teeth and lips in exasperation. "I've got to take this."

Someone on the other end was talking excitedly in Italian.

"Come on. I've got to get back to my cabin to take this," Enrique said. She followed him to his cabin on the lower deck. He opened the door, motioned toward the couch, and said, "Relax. I'll be just another minute or two. It's okay." He put his finger to his lips beckoning her to be quiet as he continued the call.

His room overlooked the rear pool. A wide sliding glass door drew in the sunset. Large dark clouds chased them from afar. The horizon disappeared with the sunset.

For a moment she had a fleeting moment of distrust. *Wait a minute*, she thought. *That's a smooth move to get me into your room.* Then she quickly banished the thought. Enrique was a real gentleman. She wasn't being played. She knew it. And if she was, she didn't care.

As she waited, it became apparent that Enrique's frustration on the phone was real. Something serious was happening. She wondered about his job and what it could mean to them.

Suddenly, Enrique shouted, "Son of a . . . Shut her down! Get security on all Level 3 entry decks!"

The loudspeakers wailed a siren. The Captain shouted over the ship speakers, "Emergency Protocols! Security crews to Deck 3! All passengers to their rooms. REPEAT. ALL passengers to your rooms!"

Tina turned towards Enrique with a look of fear.

"Tina, I want you to stay here in my room," he said. "It's safer. I have to go. I'll come for you."

This was crazy and unexpected. Tina wasn't the sit-tight type. She peered out to the deck to see what was happening and couldn't see much. She also didn't take orders well, so she slid out the door to see what was happening. The door locked behind her. She didn't have a key.

33

No Treasure for Pirates

The on-board speaker system crackled with unintelligible shouting. The couple from Room D 320 had too much to drink. As far as they could tell, they had front-row seats on a super-exciting maritime drill. They sat in their chairs on their balcony deck watching it all as if it was a TV mini drama. They were pleased with themselves and the upgrade they took for the cruise.

Cruise passengers like Stuart and Dominique were oblivious to the risk. It didn't suit cruise companies like Enrique's to over-emphasize the piracy risk. Pirates generally didn't go after cruise ships. They preferred smaller, easier-to-board ships with fewer, less-trained crew members. However, it didn't mean that ships like Enrique's were immune to the risk.

Often pirates shadowed the well-known courses of ships like the "Joys of Love" as they engaged in their high-seas treachery, feasting instead on the unsuspecting and unprepared smaller sail boats of the wealthy.

The "Joys of Love's" alarms sounded loud and clear. With all the excitement and movement on deck, the couple unwittingly sat in their chairs and watched, as if there was no danger. The truth was the opposite. Their lack of awareness and naivete placed them at incredible risk.

Enrique knew the risk. It was his job to know the perils of the maritime industry. It was the third time one of his ships had been attacked, and the second time he was on board. He knew exactly what to do.

He remembered one of his most potent life lessons: *Things go wrong all the time. It is the nature of things—to go wrong, not right. Catching those wrongs before things turn ugly is the trick.* Enrique was there to hopefully make the catch. He felt it was his calling. He had signed on for exactly this. It was a chilling responsibility and calling.

After the call, Enrique raced to the priority intercom, entered his code, A-2–111, and shouted, "Security force to weapons cache. Full arms!"

Things were moving fast. He quickly unlocked the weapons box and pulled three automatic weapons and four grenades. He secured the case. He turned on the deck lights to break the darkness and illuminate any intruders.

The grenades would provide an unpleasant surprise for the intruders if they attempted to board. Those intruders would escape to blown-up hulls of their boats. Enrique handed off two of the assault rifles to his team. They needed to quickly get in position to fend off the pirates should they make it to the deck.

The ship had rows of powerful strobe lights bouncing off the water to help ward off pirates. The lights did not deter this group of marauders. When the pirates came alongside, they threw grapple hooks to the ship's rails and climbed monkey-fast to deploy netting for their assault team.

Enrique's team knew what to do. Be in position. Anticipate. Protect their precious cargo: everyone on board. The pirates were ruthless. Shoot to kill. Maritime law allows lethal force to protect your ship. The law could not stop the lethal actions of these reckless thieves.

Under the cover of darkness and smoke bombs, two high-powered speed boats had come alongside The "Joys of Love"—one of seven Mistresses of the Sea cruise liners. Enrique hoped his crew's preparedness would be a surprise to the invaders.

Good communication was essential. There were seven team leaders, each with radios. On this cruise, he was the most experienced and led the force. Several hand-picked crew members assisted the team leads. The practice drills they had held quietly each morning had their desired effect. His team was ready.

The Captain was experienced and readied his team on the bridge. He locked the bridge down, armed his officers, and joined their ready-to-fire defense positions.

Pirates would NOT take *his* command post without meeting a volley of shots from his trained team. An attempt on his bridge would be their last living mistake.

The pirates had other plans. The bridge was not the target. Their goal was to disable the engines. They could call in more of their compadres once they had disabled the ship. Once onboard they expected to overtake an unprepared security force. With engines and communications down, the pirates could call in their compadres and loot the ship and its passengers before the Coast Guard or any other help might arrive. They expected their attack would take thirty minutes tops.

The young woman Dominique from Cabin D-320 was the first to wake from the couple's stupor as they crouched half-drunk behind the rail on the balcony outside their room. She noticed a shadowy figure creep over the ship's exterior rail thirty feet away. Fear coursed through her.

She couldn't see his face. She could see metal gleaming in the staccato strobe lights bouncing off the water below. She gripped Stuart's hand. He shivered. They didn't know what to do.

Enrique noticed the couple but couldn't reach them. The first unlucky fellow over the rail was Enrique's signal to light up the deck. The lights temporarily blinded the invaders. The devil's helper drew his pistol as he leapt onto the deck. His first shot rang out. How many more of them were coming?

Enrique's team quickly fired. There wasn't time for a civil demand for the pirates to drop their guns. One of the pirates threw a smoke grenade. The "Joys of Love" was under attack and in chaos.

To Enrique's great surprise and distress, he caught sight of Tina on the deck near the couple. His heart sank. What was she thinking? "God dammit!"

Two other pirates jumped the rails behind Tina. "Tina, watch out!" Enrique yelled.

She turned quickly, saw the pirates, and instinctively shot the closest person coming at her. As he fell, she jumped up onto the balcony where the couple was.

Enrique couldn't believe his eyes.

Enrique's team wasted no time. They sprayed the rails and the deck with bullets. Anyone coming over would lose their life. The scene unfolding before them was terrifying. The pirates scrambled back. Some fell into the water. Some fell down into their boats.

This wasn't the plan of El Diablo, the head of the pirate crew. His victory celebration and all the jewelry and money had not made it into their backpacks. He would be famous back home, but not for the reasons he had planned.

El Diablo's story had changed.

El Diablo De Cuatro Dedos

Juan Pedro grew up on the docks of El Rote. The young men he hung around with would become his crew. None of them were meant to be engineers or doctors, or even deck hands for a cruise ships. Those young men there were destined for crime and El Rote's sick version of glory.

You couldn't blame the young men for the choices they made. They came from El Rote Cay—the harbor of rot.

Little Juan Pedro didn't know how he got there, or why he followed Poi, the fisherman. Juan Pedro was an abandoned child. His parents were killed in a turf war when their sailboat was overtaken at sea by pirates.

He had royal blood through his parents, but it didn't matter. In the school of life, royalty sat in the back with everyone else. His family only knew that he, his parents, and the sailboat had disappeared—maybe forever.

Juan Pedro looked up to the fisherman. Dock life was all he knew. Most of the fisherman there had a limp, or a lost arm, a slashed face, or a twisted back. Perhaps they were caught in a fishing net, a bar fight gone too far, or a swinging boom crushed them to the side of steel hulled ship. Misfits of misfortune they were. That was Juan Pedro's destiny too.

To learn his skills on the water Juan Pedro did what he was told. He felt lucky to go out on the boats. He loved to fish. He loved to steal.

El Rote Cay was not one of those elegant, cruise-ship owned islands with coconut decorated beer bars, sandy beaches, bikini-clad women, colorful kayaks, and jet skis laying on the sand. This Cay was a cauldron of contamination tucked away in a tiny group of islands rimmed by trees that hid oil-slicked water, floating debris, and dead animals. You couldn't see the bottom at even three feet. The stench made you want to vomit, unless you were from El Rote. El Rote's "citizens" had grown used to the smell—like not being able to smell your own house when others clearly could smell it.

The smell traveled with the men in and out of jails. Women on the edge would try to pull them back to a semi-normal life with a family that could soften them. But not Juan Pedro and not Poi. They were drawn to the "bad life" at the edge of danger, always in the water.

Their devils could not be tamed.

Poi had taken a shine to Juan Pedro. The little boy was spry, part fish and part dolphin, part man and part boy. Juan Pedro climbed the masts like a gymnast and dove into the water to retrieve anything. He could fish too. When Juan Pedro caught a glimpse of a movement in the water below, he would grab his net and hook, dive deep to the bottom, and tickle the back of an unsuspecting flounder until they lifted out of the bottom sand and darted into his net. With his catch, the boy shot out of the water screaming with joy. His eyes were so used to the salt that he didn't use goggles. He could see underwater without them.

Poi watched over Juan Pedro.

One day approaching the winter, Poi called Juan Pedro, "We fish the outer reef today."

Juan Pedro excitedly jumped from an old barrel eight feet away, grabbed a loose rope and swung onto the ship. They were headed to a sandy bar where the fish were usually plentiful.

The poles had to be held tightly in place. "Juan Pedro," Poi shouted. "Watch the lines. Your fingers will pay the price. You are not a lobster. Fingers don't grow back."

It was an old line repeated time and again. Juan Pedro heard it in his sleep: *They don't grow back.*

Juan Pedro usually listened. But on this day a seagull caught little Juan Pedro's eye. The bird darted toward his head. He lost track of the line being pulled by a large fish. His baby finger caught the line and was pulled quickly into the reel.

In a split second his finger held motionless at the reel. In slow motion, the fish, the line, the boat riding the swells, and Juan Pedro's finger were at odds. Then horribly his finger snapped and was severed at the base of his fist. Juan Pedro screamed more from fear than pain at this point. Poi ran over. Together, they watched his finger drop into the water below. Blood poured from the stub of his finger over his bare feet.

For a moment, his finger sat on the surface of the water and then disappeared, fluttering its way to the bottom, taking with it the little remaining innocence Juan Pedro had.

Poi grabbed an oily fish rag and covered Juan Pedro's hand. He needed alcohol and stitches to suture the stub of Juan Pedro's finger. Poi had several nips of vodka in his pocket. He took one, quickly twisted the cover off, and forced the little bottle on Juan Pedro's knuckle. The alcohol burned but it would prevent infection. The vodka turned milky red.

Poi looked down at him in disgust. "Stupid boy. We could have lost the catch."

Juan Pedro wore the bottle until they got back to the dock. There were no hospitals, no urgent care, and no doctors on El Rote Cay. Poi stitched the boy up with a fishing line.

El Diablo de cuatro dedos was born; the four-fingered devil had arrived.

The savage fishing boats had simply charged another harsh penalty for another careless newbie. What other scars did the boats have in store for El Diablo? The stern message of amputation kept him safe for many years, but it also cut off any softness and decency the boy had.

El Diablo used his anger to fuel his conquests. El Diablo, Juan Pedro's nickname, was a testament to his career of violence. He wasn't just a petty thief. He was dark—determined to make his mark and set himself apart from his fellow pirates and thieves in their hidden Cay. The four-fingered devil was vicious like the sea itself. He told everyone from the time he was five years old that he would take down a cruise ship.

They laughed. That is until he and his crew took down a sixty-five-foot sailboat with a crew of seven. He taunted the boat's Captain by cutting a finger off his hand. "You see, you are like me now! And lucky to be alive!"

He cast an evil and scornful look at the man as he said, "It won't grow back."

Then he gangplanked the entire crew one hundred meters from shore and brought the ship back to El Rote to a hero's welcome amongst his thieving sailors. His next target was a five hundred-ton cargo ship with a crew of ten. Three of their crew gave up their lives for the privilege of meeting *El Diablo de cuatro dedos* at sea.

Back at the ship, the on-board speaker system on the "Joys of Love" crackled with unintelligible shouting. Juan Pedro was making his move. He wanted everyone to know his name. The "Joys of Love" was his first great conquest. From this day on, he would strike fear wherever he went. To gain loyalty from his crew, he was reckless and fearless. He led the charge. True to his ruthless destiny, he was the first to charge up and over the rails of the cruise ship.

He would meet his destiny!

35

El Diablo Meets Tina

Tina heard Enrique scream. Afraid, she quickly pulled her .38 caliber from her pocketbook. Tina was a sure shot. Her dad, bless his soul, had taken her hunting and to the shooting range more times than anything else they did together. It bonded them— the tough police officer and his "innocent," soft-hearted daughter. They practiced simulations at the range and in video games. Their super-hero video game fun gave them super smiles and super confidence.

At Enrique's scream, Tina turned and instinctively shot the closest person coming at her. As he fell, she jumped up onto the balcony where a couple hid in terror.

El Diablo's story changed when he met Tina's cold bullet. She was a sure shot and not afraid to use the gun in her purse. That prescription saved her life and changed his forever.

Tina spun around to a wild-eyed, screaming banshee with a knife gripped in his mouth. El Diablo leapt over the rails in frantic furor. He attacked. It wasn't personal. If you got in his way, you were dead! That's all.

It wasn't personal for Tina either. She fired quickly. She caught El Diablo in the right chest just above his heart. He staggered in disbelief and pain. His eyes shouted the unfairness of his broken dream.

Enrique couldn't believe his eyes. His mind raced. *Tina had a gun?* He sensed she was a gamer, but her self-defense bordered on crazy.

Enrique's team wasted no time. They sprayed the rails and the deck with bullets. Anyone coming over the rails would likely be killed or wounded and driven into the sea. The scene unfolding before them was terrifying.

Tina quickly took aim at the next unsavory character to raise his head above the rail and disposed of him. A second pirate met his fate at Tina's feet. The battle for the ship was on. The deck was chaos. Smoke and senseless screams filled the air. Enrique's crew engaged the remaining pirates. The pirates lost their chance. Tina played an unexpected part in the real-life drama. The element of surprise, the tactical play, worn by Enrique and his well-drilled team.

Manuel, a short, stocky, well-built member of Enrique's security team launched a grenade at the escaping speedboat below. The ensuing blast shattered the back of the boat. Two unlucky pirates were shot skyward and fell into the water below. They sloshed back and forth, lifeless in the waves.

The second ship sped away. Only half of the attacking pirates made it back on board.

Several of the pirates were shot on the way up. Shot and wounded, they fell back and got tangled in the climbing ropes. They hung un-flag-like against the ship. Blood dripped into the water below turning the water from a spotlight-bouncing, soft-blue color into a sickening wine-red color, a symbol of the mistake the episode had become for El Diablo and his crew of unlucky pirates. Blood stained El Diablo's hands. His best friend was dead. El Diablo was hanging on for his life as his speedboat pounded the waves in furious retreat to El Rote.

Desperation hung on him like the dark clouds of an ocean storm on the distant horizon. His crew sat in stunned disbelief holding to the shattered edge of the boat. Poi waited at the dock. As the boat came into view at full speed, Poi's sixth sense spread over him. He could feel the trouble for his devil friend. It felt the same on the day El Diablo earned his nickname.

Back on the "Joys of Love," an eerie and uncomfortable quiet settled on the ship. Tina leaned back in a corner out of sight to take a breath and gather herself. Passengers slowly wandered out of their rooms to the deck rails to see what had happened. It was too soon for the "All Clear" order.

Enrique grabbed the microphone and shouted: "Code Three! Code Three! Get back in your rooms. The deck is not safe."

Fifteen long minutes later, after a sweep of the deck by his crew, Enrique gave the "All Clear" signal and handed the microphone to his lead com officer. The ship blared three, long, triumphant blasts to signal the danger had passed.

A long day of review was ahead, but first Enrique had to find Tina. She had some serious 'splainin' to do.

36

The Truth About Enrique

Enrique gathered his team for head counts and to re-group. Cigarettes and top-shelf whiskey passed freely to the crew. He dispensed with his administrative work as quickly as possible. He couldn't wait to get to Tina.

Enriques' second in command asked the question everyone wanted the answer to. "Chief, who is the broad with the gun?"

Enrique smiled. "Can't say as I know." With a nod he replied, "I'll find out though."

They both laughed.

Enrique couldn't get Tina and her sharp-shooting, cowboy-like image out of his mind. The crew spent a short time celebrating. Enrique hoisted a shot of his smoothest Bullet Redemption Rye and toasted his crew, signaling a back-to-work re-set. After assigning clean-up responsibilities, his crew would reconvene at 0800 hours the following day.

Enrique raced off to find Tina.

Back in her room Tina was writing a letter to her mom and dad. Writing to her loved ones was one way Tina processed her experiences. It gave her time and space to understand what happened.

Dear Mom and Dad,

You won't believe this. The night started out fun. But then our ship was attacked by pirates. That guy I told you about, Enrique—the one I wanted to know more about—well, I found out lots more about him today and about me. The experience was a real-life, adventure movie, and I was the femme fatal. Believe it or not, I saved us at gunpoint. And Enrique is some kind of a security specialist. I don't know what kind yet, but I'm going to find out when I meet him. I'm putting it to him. I want the answers. Even more than you do.

Our ship was sailing slowly to our next port when an alarm went off. All the deck lights came on. Everyone was ordered to their cabins. Sirens blared. None of us passengers knew what was happening. When I came out to check for myself, I saw this couple on a deck just a few feet below my deck and climbed down to them and stashed myself out of sight on their deck.

Dad, don't worry. I had my .38. The next thing I know, a wild-eyed, long-haired, pirate-looking-guy with a knife in his mouth comes up over the rail and lunges at us.

Dad, do you remember those video games we used to play together? And that firing range we'd go to on Saturdays?

Well, that was time well-spent. I said more "Jesus Christs"
than a church full of Catholics on Easter Sunday.
Believe it or not, I shot the guy—a pirate I guess—top right
center like we always practiced. There is mor . . .

Her thoughts were interrupted by a knock at the door. Tina yelled, "Who is it?"

"It's me. Enrique."

She looked out the little brass-rimmed, peep hole to make sure it was him, and opened the door. They fell into each other's arms. The invisible wall between them melted away. Relief from the life-threatening action just moments before engulfed them. Fast breaths. Hugs. Kisses. Her bed just feet away. His chained libido— no longer chained.

When they first met, she had stung him with her butterfly-like beauty. Enrique's awkward stumble into Tina was a distant memory. Now he felt like a swash-buckling conquistador. Tina felt the same. They were a team.

Since their first meeting, his cautious admiration had been scripted and chained by a fear of cancellation. Now those concerns fell away.

Time stripped Tina and Enrique's concerns of their power. Their pent-up emotions collided in a magical embrace. Their bodies were like unrestrained water pummeling down a waterfall to a churning base. Each of them was unwilling to let go of the other. Gripping their arms, they bounced as if dancing out questions until they tripped onto the bed and fell over.

"My God. What the hell was that?" Tina shrieked at Enrique.

"Never mind what that was," Enrique replied. "You're the one who has got some explaining to do. I've never seen a passenger do that. I don't even know if the guys on my team could have done what you did."

He held Tina out at arms' length and looked into her eyes. "How did you know what to do?" he asked.

"I just reacted," she said. "It happened so quickly. My dad used to emphasize the three P's: practice and preparation pay off."

Enrique pulled Tina close again. "Well good for you," he said. "And good for your dad. It was incredible. I think you saved your life, and the couple on that deck too. Your shots triggered our crew into action. I'm very proud of you."

Tina took a breath. Their bodies were still pinned to each other, and for a brief moment she imagined they could remain like that forever. But, then she recognized she needed something more. She slipped from Enrique's embrace.

"Not so fast Enrique. You have some explaining to do, too," she said. "You told me you had an interest in the ship. I want to know more. I've earned it. Exactly what is your role here? Are you the security team lead?"

Enrique gulped. He couldn't hold Tina off any longer. "Ummm. Not really," he said.

He cleared his throat before continuing. Finally, he blurted out, "So the thing is . . . I am part owner of the ship."

"Whaaat?" Tina intoned incredulously.

Of all the things she expected to hear, "owner" was not one of them. Her earlier inquiries hinted at nothing more than whispers about Enrique being a celebrity. No one knew or shared any more about him on the ship, in spite of her multiple attempts to find information about him.

He had the perfect disguise, Old Stumble-and-Fall. She remembered him falling into her when they first met. She grinned, smiling secretly to herself.

Enrique decided to let things simmer. He smiled and said, "What do you say we get a bite to eat. I'm starving. Let's do a sit-down dinner. I know one of the chefs."

Tina wrinkled her nose and gave him her corkscrew look. "No kidding," she said.

Enrique said, "I have a few things to attend to. Meet me in the Captains Lounge on deck six in a half hour. I'll get us a table and we can talk about anything you want."

"Anything?" Tina asked.

Enrique nodded. He owed her that much. "Anything you'd like," he said.

37

Enrique's Hidden Story

Tina looked in her closet. What should she wear? It seemed like such a trivial concern now. After a life-threatening pirate attack, fashion seemed less important than ever. Yet thinking back when she packed for the trip, she had laid out all her clothes on her bed at home—carefully choosing what would make her look her best. Shorts, blouses, bathing suits, two nice dresses, shoes, and seven pairs of sexy underwear just in case.

She chuckled to herself. Should she bother to dress to impress? Or keep it plain and simple for Enrique.

She chose her red shorts and a sheer, see-through pink blouse—and yes, the sexy, lace pink underwear.

Enrique wore khaki shorts with a collared white shirt. His four gold wire stripes adorned his Captain's insignia badge. His name was printed on the chest pocket in gold braided letters. It was formal and classy. He no longer hid his identity from her.

The two of them fit like a hand in a glove. It was obvious as they walked arm-in-arm to the maître d station. The maître d wore a crisp white uniform with a single gold tassel on his left shoulder.

"Sir, your table is ready," said the maître d as he led them to a table overlooking the bow of the ship. There were multiple guards on duty—as Enrique had directed. He wasn't sure if there were more attacks planned. Perhaps there was a network of thieves. No matter. His ship would be ready.

Enrique followed the maître d with Tina latched on his arm. He couldn't help but think of Marilyn. After her death, Enrique had thrown himself into the business. He was obsessed. All the work helped to keep him from thinking about her, which is something he didn't want to do. But now as he felt Tina on his arm, he eased out a quiet sigh. This "date" was a big step for Enrique.

As they approached the table, Enrique swept his arm toward the table and offered Tina a choice of where to sit. He learned to do this long ago. It was a way to show respect for whomever he was with. By his design, Tina would choose their seats. So many of his peers would simply grab the seat of their choice. His habit was a small thing—but important. She took the seat looking over the bow and the light fog-covered sunset. He took the seat with his back to the bow but could see the bar and the patrons of the restaurant. He liked the result. He felt good that Tina had a view she liked, and he could see the environment. Old habits die hard. He liked the security of seeing his surroundings.

"Okay, Miss Sure-Shot. Fire away," said Enrique.

Tina laughed. Tina loved Enrique's taunting playful manner. Banter was important to her. It provided the back and forth for someone to be her equal. She was competitive. She needed that outlet. It was refreshing to her.

She had multiple questions for Enrique. Some were about the event they both endured and witnessed. *Why were they attacked? Did any passengers from the ship get hurt? Who were the people who attacked them?*

She had questions about Enrique, too. *Why the cloak and dagger approach? Was he attached to anyone? What did Roberto (Enrique's son) know about her?*

Not all the questions were for Enrique. She had deep thoughts and concerns of her own. *How had their paths had crossed. What devil or angel put them together?*

She looked at his left hand and noticed his gold wedding band. Not a good sign. *Let's start with that*, she thought.

She didn't know exactly how to address it: "Alright, Enrique, your wedding band is screaming at me right now."

He answered immediately. "When Marilyn died, I couldn't bring myself to take the ring off. I don't know when that will happen."

Tina didn't love his answer, but she appreciated his honesty. She continued with the questions.

"Why are you so secretive about your position and who you are?" she asked.

The answer was obvious to Enrique. "I don't want the spotlight on what I do, or the work that goes with the job title," he responded. "I like to be in the background. I can better gauge what is going when I'm—let's call it, undercover, or in the background—sort of un-fettered."

This made sense to Tina. "Yeah, Okay, I can see that," she agreed."

"You said you were part owner. That seems a broad title. Can you explain that a bit more?" she asked. The journalist in her was at work, and Enrique felt like he was on trial.

"Is this an inquisition?

She barked back, "You said ANY question."

"Fair enough. Fair enough," Enrique admitted with a smile.

As they bantered back and forth, their waiter appeared and commanded their attention. "What will you be ordering to drink, Miss?"

Realizing she hadn't even looked at the menu, she asked for a few more minutes.

"Would you like the sommelier's suggestion?" the waiter offered.

"That won't be necessary," said Enrique. Instead, he ordered a bottle of Italian Reserve with a hint of blackberry and plum flavor. He had a meticulous command of the wines the ship carried.

Once the waiter left, Enrique continued. "So, the cruise line is part of our family's business."

Tina let the words soak in. "Part of it?" she asked.

"Yeah, we do publishing, and we own a few vineyards to supply our ships with great wine."

Tina's head was spinning. *Ships (more than one). Vineyards? Publishing?*

"Enrique, what are you telling me?"

"What do you mean?" Enrique replied.

"Well, not everyone speaks of 'multiple vineyards' and 'ships' as if they were coins in their pockets."

"Yeah, I guess that's true enough," Enrique realized. He wished he had been more discreet, but also realized Tina deserved to know the truth. "Does it bother you that much?"

Tina wasn't sure how to respond. She paused for a minute before saying, "No. I think it takes a little getting used to—if you know what I mean," Tina responded.

Before they could engage further on the topic of his business, a cat caught Enrique's attention. "That damn Flora May and her cats," said Enrique.

Tina swung around in her chair and caught a glimpse of the black cat with the spooky yellow eyes. "You know Flora May?

"Well, of course, I do. I hired her," said Enrique.

"Oh, my goodness. She's amazing," Tina said. "I saw her on my second day on board. She was mesmerizing and her predictions . . ." Tina realized Flora May's predictions sat across the table from her. "Well, they came true."

Flora May came by their table chasing her cat. "Look who we have here," she said in a smarmy, self-satisfied way. "Oh, dearie me, Tina. What a nice, attractive outfit you have on," Flora May said as she peered down at Tina's blouse with a knowing grin.

Enrique was impatient. "Flora May, get your damn cats out of here."

Flora May was not the least concerned about decorum and quickly spat back, "Don't you sass talk me or I'll make your ears turn green and your breath so bad you'll never see this little dearie again."

They all broke into laughter. Tina thought back to her mom's advice. You'll know THE ONE. In so many ways, Enrique felt right. He had a way of people. He didn't take himself too seriously. Tina was starting to think that her mom might like him. She sure did.

38

Flora May's Arrow Hit the Mark

After Flora May shuffled off, Enrique looked deep into Tina's eyes. She didn't flinch. He had only a few dates prior to meeting Tina. Not a single one of those women could look into his eyes without getting uncomfortable.

Not Tina. Her eyes pierced through the shield of his often-stern eyes as the edge of her mouth curled up to mock him.

She was a fighter. That was a sure bet.

Unintentionally, his thoughts escaped to his late wife. Was it Flora May's prodding? His own thoughts were strange. *What happened to those we bury. He didn't know why but his mind was racing. What is on the other side? Do bad people get their just desserts? Or is there a truly merciful God that forgives all indiscretions? Is that the Final Design? Or does the burning hell of our nightmares consume those we deem to "deserve" what they get?*

Pushing these thoughts aside, Enrique didn't know what to expect from his time with Tina. His thoughts weren't exactly an inspiration.

He wasn't the only one drifting off. Tina's mind wasn't quite right either. Her eyes were shut as she envisioned a giant dance floor and Enrique's outstretched arms. She could barely shake herself free of her little dream. She forced herself to back to Enrique and their celebratory dinner. She felt closer to him than ever. It was a good feeling. She took a deep inhale of the raspberry plum wine and closed her eyes to bring herself into the moment.

When she opened her eyes, Enrique was smiling a content smile. His eyes had softened. She was beginning to think he was "The One."

A small fireplace video lit up a screen to their left and bounced flame-like shadows off Tina's sheer pink top and smooth cheeks.

"My gosh—you look really good," Enrique said.

"Yeah?" she questioned with a bit of a blush as she curled her lower lip over her bottom teeth. It was an old, amusing habit she had when she was nervous. Enrique delighted in observing her slight discomfort.

Enrique felt like he could swallow her whole dessert-like sweetness. His emotions ran high. Tina tried to think of a question. She didn't know why. Love was hanging in the air. She couldn't decide whether to pluck it out of the air and blow him a kiss or extinguish her discomfort by firing off more questions to get the promised answers she wanted.

The waiter came back to take their order and, for the moment, she was rescued.

She fumbled bleary eyed over the menu choices before deciding on the roast duck and a Caesar salad topped with avocado and raspberries. She knew she couldn't go wrong.

"That's a fine choice." said Enrique.

Tina took a sip of her wine before launching into the next line of questioning. "So here we are," she said. "Two reckless souls with a connection. What's next for us?"

"Like everything in life that is worthwhile, you work and wait," Enrique responded in a semi-foolish, guru-like, oft-handed way before he paused and giggled to show that he knew the silliness of his "b.s." answer. It was a fun tease. They both laughed.

A two-person band started playing romantic Italian songs out on the deck. The music drifted to their table. "The music is lovely," commented Tina.

"I hoped you would like it," Enrique said. "I play those songs all the time in the evening. They bring me the comfort of home."

"Where's home?"

Enrique sighed and smiled slightly as he thought about his favorite place. "Outside of Pisa in the Tuscany region of Italy. It is a beautiful place filled with Mediterranean influences. There's vegetation everywhere and beautiful architecture. Great stone buildings. Villas and gardens and lovely meadows."

Tina tried to picture his home in her mind. She imagined them together in Tuscany.

The waiter appeared with their meal. The presentation was exquisite. The multi-colored salad was topped with bright-green, large avocado slices. Black and red raspberries circled the rim of the plate in clock-like fashion—red on the hour and black meticu-lously placed in between each hour spot.

Tina's duck was roasted to perfection. Enrique had a simple, medium-rare steak cooked in the chef's special family-recipe sauce. It was a unique flavor that could not be had elsewhere.

An unmistakable crisp, salt-water mist filled their lungs. The smell in the air dared you to breathe more deeply than ever.

"So tell me more about what you do—please," said Tina.

"Ah—a bit of everything. Just management," said Enrique, not wanting to break the magic of the moment with his work-life story. "I'm just a problem-finder and an occasional problem-solver." He hoped to steer the conversation away from business and into a more intimate direction.

"So, I have to fight for every answer?" Tina intoned.

"Okay, okay, okay, it's just that I feel like we'd be wasting our precious time on boring work talk," said Enrique.

"Well, it's not boring to me," Tina countered.

Enrique started to explain. "I make routine calls to our group of ships to check on security issues, staffing needs, supply issues, and. . ."

Tina interrupted him. She negated her first answer. "You are right. That is boring!"

They both laughed heartily.

Their desserts came. Enrique said, "Let's take the desserts back to my suite."

Her stomach tingled as she answered, "That's a great idea."

His eyes lit up as he nodded excitedly and led the way.

When they arrived at the room, in just seconds the door unlocked itself, the desserts escaped their hands onto the kitchen table. Their arms entangled in a fast-moving embrace. Their hands searched for an end point their fingers didn't know. Their fingers couldn't rest. A passionate kiss froze their lips together for just long enough before a reckless abandonment controlled not only them but everything in the room. Sheets pulled themselves back, pillows jumped onto the floor, blankets slid, lights shut off by themselves, mirrors lit the room, doors opened then shut, music played, clothing fell to the floor, glasses jumped to the nightstands. Everything in the room danced in a cacophony of movements. Sweet inner clothing lifted tornado-like into the air as their bodies crashed furiously together in a scramble, a crescendo, a breathless climax, and then—just as quickly—stillness.

Eyes that had locked shut got permission to open. The cigarette on the counter lit itself and smoked. A word barely passed their lips before they sank into a restful sleep—arm in arm—dreaming.

Enrique's phone woke them from their sweat-induced slumber.

"Got it! I'm on my way."

"Really? Tina said, looking over the sheets in disbelief.

"Yup. You wanted to know what I do. Come with me."

"Okay, I guess." Tina's answer surprised both of them. She jumped out of bed. Her clothing—still in the soft evening trance— quickly jumped onto her body. She fixed her top, brushed her hair and said, "I'm ready."

Enrique, still fumbling with his shirt buttons, was ecstatic. This could be fun. He glanced at his watch and noted Tina's efficient jumpstart. Two minutes and eighteen seconds. That works! They busted out of the room and ran up to the com deck under a gorgeous early morning sunrise.

Tina's new job awaited.

39

Tina's New Job

When they got in the com room, Enrique chuckled. "You'll have to fill out an application," he said.

"What for?" Tina replied playfully.

"We are offering you a job. You are going to be my new assistant," Enrique beamed.

"Are you kidding me?" Tina looked at him intensely.

"Come on. Quick! We are in a hurry. I'll explain."

Up in the com room at the bridge, with Tina in tow, Enrique asked the chief engineer for the latest report relating to their earlier urgent call. The chief engineer, Mark Siemex, was six-foot-three-inches tall with a short, well-trimmed, half-grey moustache—no beard. He had a Leatherman multi-tool on his belt, a giant 24-hour diver's watch on his left wrist, and a pressed, wrinkle-free white shirt with a blue badge carrying three yellow stripes on his left sleeve. In his shirt pocket rode his good luck leprechaun chain (no one knew) and a push-button, retractable, ultra-thin, pen and pencil gadget (for architects and engineers only).

Mark responded to Enrique, "It looks like our "Splendid Romance" has pulled up some kind of cable in St. Maarten outside of Philipsburg."

"Thanks, chief. Get Captain Jillean on the line."

Enrique grabbed the #9 ship's radio from the charging station and handed it to Tina. "Use this. Press #6 to reach me. Let everyone know you are #9. I'll be with the Captain on the bridge making plans for our SXM trip."

In minutes the chief engineer put Captain Jillean through to Enrique.

Captain Jillean was a good-looking, smart, small-framed woman who was a technical marvel with computer navigation systems. "CJ," as she was called by her team, always carried a heavy-duty, half-inch elastic band. Her signature bad habit was to twist the half-inch band between her left thumb and her index finger, and to aim it menacingly at her team.

In meetings she methodically wrapped and unwrapped the band around her thumb and over her index finger. Her fingers never slept. She appeared lost in thought. That is until she snapped the band at any one she thought wasn't paying attention—especially if they were using their phone. People in her command quickly learned "Verboten" for phone use during meetings.

Everyone chuckled when a newcomer got whacked by the inevitable elastic slingshot. CJ would always have this faux hurt expression on her face for having to discipline the offender. Her team knew she secretly loved the startling effect.

CJ's remote troubleshooting abilities were legend in the company. Her expertise had helped Enrique and the Arnoldos build their business through hard times when they purchased and ran their very first, large cruise ship thirty years earlier, "The Lovely Maiden." She was a sporty 700 feet, with a one-hundred-sixty-foot beam, seven guest decks, and gross tonnage of just 105,600. She carried 1,100 passengers and 550 crew members.

"The Lovely Maiden" was the ship that leap-frogged their company into being a world-class cruise company with international routes serving Europe, the Americas, and beyond.

The "Maiden" was a great ship, but as good as she was, she was a poor sister to their second large cruise ship the "Joys of Love." It operated with a crew of 1675, a length of 985 feet, 185,000 tons, and a capacity of 3,800 passengers.

Captain Jillean took on the captaincy of "The Splendid Romance" when the Arnoldos retired "The Lovely Maiden" after a 33-year run with the company.

"Jillean, old friend, how are you?" asked Enrique.

"We're okay—just aggravated that we're delayed by this underground cable. A trawler might have dragged the cable in near us. There's nothing showing it on our maps," she said.

"Okay. Fair enough," said Enrique. "I'm handing you over to my assistant, Tina. Give her a list of what your needs are. We'll be in SXM in 24."

Tina's life was traveling at the speed of sound. Or was it light speed?

Thrilled didn't begin to describe her feelings. She loved the adventure of life on a cruise ship—the pace, and the excitement. She could barely keep up. Perfect! A new love? And an adventure-filled job? Was this her calling?

She didn't know. She felt an inner calmness to her experience in spite of the chaos surrounding them all. She understood now what professional athletes described as slowing down the tempo of the game at critical points.

"Tina, take Captain Jillean's call and find out what she needs," commanded Enrique.

Enrique handed Tina the phone.

Tina jumped right in. Enrique's assessment of her was correct. She was a gamer and could hit the ground running on any project.

"Hi, Captain Jillean. What's your most pressing need?" Tina asked.

Captain Jillean requested a contact at the St. Maarten port authority. Captain Jillean also needed to confirm the authorized "messaging" to be shared with the passengers about the broken-cable incident and the potential delay. The second request was right up Tina's alley. Tina was a good writer, and as a passenger she could address passenger needs with uncommon sensitivity.

Tina asked Captain Jillean, "How long of a delay do you expect?"

Captain Jillean responded, "We have to find the origin of the cable and inspect for any damage to our ship, the cable, and the environment. I'm guessing 12 to 24 hours if everything goes well. Based on our underwater cameras, we think the wires endangering our props could be from a ripped cable dragged in from a trawler or another ship. But we have to be sure the cable strands are completely disengaged from our ship before we head back out to sea."

"Please hold on a second, Captain Jillean," Tina said.

She pressed #6. "Enrique, Captain Jillean needs a contact for the harbormaster at Philipsburg in St. Marteen."

Enrique returned, "I got it covered, and I've got a salvage guy who works out of Simpson Bay mid-island. My friend Rolando knows the harbormaster in SXM. Let Jillean know we'll have a team working this problem within eight hours."

Tina returned to Captain Jillean. "We'll have a contact for you at the port in my next com on this shift," Tina said. "Our dive team will be on site with you in eight hours—at approximately 0600 hours." Tina continued, "I'll work on the passenger communication and have it over to you in an hour."

The chief engineer looked over at his first assistant James, nodded at Tina, and whispered, "She's a sharp one, eh?"

James replied, "Yeah, I think she's the one who shot the first pirates over the rail on deck three."

"That was pretty incredible stuff. One of our cameras caught her spinning and firing at point blank range into the first bastard up. He got a surprise even the devil himself couldn't predict."

"Yo, yeah," replied the chief. "She'll be a great addition to our team."

"No wonder #6 wants her on the team. She's got balls."

The com office radio crackled. "Send Tina to the bridge." Tina recognized the voice as #6.

"He's waiting Miss . . . " The chief's voice trailed off slightly not knowing how to address her.

"Tina. You can call me Tina or #9."

Awkwardly he responded, "Yes, sir—Miss #9."

The chief pointed to the side door and directed Tina to take the third vertical ladder on her right up to the bridge. "Hustle. He doesn't like to wait," the chief said.

The chief grabbed his radio, held down #6 and said, "Nine is on the way, sir."

Tina smiled at the chief and hurried out, and up the square plated steps of the ladder. The steps were spaced about 12 inches apart and off set from the wall just enough to allow a full landing of your shoes. You had to be in shape to climb the vertical ship ladders. She was. The rails alongside the stairs were primer grey and round. She jumped up two steps at a time. Excitement coursed through her veins. She counted eighteen rungs to the bridge. The top of the ladder extended four feet above the deck.

When she arrived, Enrique opened the door and greeted her with a warm welcome and an introduction. "Captain, this is Tina. She's #9 on our ship radios."

The Captain of the ship she was on reached out to shake her hand. "Tina, I've heard a lot about you. Welcome to the team," she said.

"Happy to meet you, Captain," Tina replied.

Captain Johann Berks was a stocky man with short white hair, and a scar on his right cheek that stretched over his cheekbone. Twenty years earlier, an operation had put his brutally injured jaw back in place. It made him scowl even if he wasn't trying. Most people kept their distance from the old man.

Without ever saying a word, his facial expression screamed, "No nonsense on my watch!" Tina wanted to ask him about his face, but it wasn't the right time.

Captain Berks asked, "When did you join us?"

Tina said, "Technically, not yet. We haven't really discussed terms—pay and such. So I'm not sure." He liked her candor. No nonsense.

Enrique jumped in. "If I can talk her into it, Tina will be working with me on special projects effective immediately."

The Captain looked at Tina and replied, "He doesn't usually take 'no' for an answer. I imagine your conversation won't be any different."

Enrique smiled.

Tina turned to Enrique, "So *this* is what you do?"

Enrique said, "Yes. Problems find me, and then I find solutions. I'd like you to be one of my solutions. I need a 'right hand' with a different set of skills than we typically utilize on board."

He turned to Johann, "Captain, is our transport to the airport ready?"

Captain Berks's right index finger brushed his scarred cheek. It was his "thought stroke." Some people touch the tip of their nose when their brain is trying to unscramble things. Others look up at the ceiling. His "scar-touch" was an easy way to tell he was trying to figure things out. He started rubbing that scar years ago after the knife wound healed. He sustained the injury after rescuing a giant sea turtle from a fishing net off the shore of Bermuda. The turtle swiped at the tangled net to free himself causing Captain Berks to jab his own cheekbone.

The Arnoldo company took excellent care of Captain Berks as he recovered from the injury. He was a company lifer from then on. He and Enrique knew each other well. Their years of dependability built enormous trust between them.

"The transport team will be here in 30 minutes," the Captain responded.

Captain Berks turned to Tina. "Okay, #9. Go pack your gear. I'll have a mate at your room to move your gear to transport in 20 minutes.

Tina looked at the three of them—Enrique, the Captain, and the chief engineer. She took a deep breath. Granny was right. She did know "The One." She had found her way. Tina's appreciation of her Granny "moment" was short-lived.

Enrique barked. "Let's go #9. We've got a plane to catch."

She smiled at him and said, "Yes, sir."

They enjoyed their playful numbering system. Others on the ship caught on.

Enrique said, "Use Code 69 for my suite." She rolled her eyes. She knew exactly what he meant.

She ran off to her room and grabbed her things. She threw her hastily packed bag over her shoulder, and raced off to Enrique's suite. She dialed in the code "69." The door unlocked. Time passed quickly as she scrambled to grab her things and erase evidence of their steam-filled night. Enrique's things were already packed. She barely got back to her room when the mate knocked. "I'm here for your luggage, #9."

She told the mate, "I need a couple of minutes."

She scrambled to check her bed and drawers to make sure nothing was left behind. She remembered the time on a vacation cruise when she left three pairs of brand-new shorts in the lower drawer of the bureau in her room. Not a good memory.

Then Tina called her mom.

"Hi, Mom. I miss you. I have so much to tell you," Tina gushed.

Tina's mom answered excitedly. "Oh, Tina. I love you. How are you? I haven't heard from you in four days. What happened? Why didn't you call? Are you okay?"

"Yes, Mom. Yes! Mom! I'm better than okay. Too much to tell. I'm rushing for a plane. Gosh, I don't know where to start. But I'm in a hurry. I'm taking a job here on the ship. Well, not exactly this ship. It's the whole fleet. We'll have to talk more later. Love you, Mom. Hugs to Dad, too."

Tina's mom was stunned. And she didn't know even half of the story. Tina made a note to call her mom again as soon as things settled on their upcoming trip to SXM.

As she settled in her seat next to Enrique on the flight to St. Maarten, she rehearsed how she would tell her mom the news.

40

Mom, I've Got Great News?

Tina went back and forth on what part to tell her mom first. She thought her mom would generally think the news was good. But she knew it wouldn't take long for her to realize that Tina was taking an "away" job. She'd always wanted to travel the world.

She still wasn't sure how her mom would feel about Enrique's age. How old was he? She decided to ask. She hadn't thought about his actual age until this moment.

Tina had already decided to take the job with the Arnoldo cruise line. Enrique was offering her an unbeatable opportunity. It was her dream job. The money almost didn't matter.

"So, here's the ticket, Mom." *No, that won't work. Too chummy.*

"Mom, do you remember that time when . . ." *Eh, too vague.*

"I fell in love, Mom." *Too direct and a bit ahead of myself too.*

"Mom, I have to tell you something. Wait, is Granny there? I've got great news for Granny." *Too tricky.*

"Mom, you won't believe what happened!" *Too cryptic.*

"Mom, I miss you and can't wait to tell you . . ." *Too long.*

Tina thought to herself as she dialed up her mom and crossed her fingers. *Well, here goes nothing. Bombs away.*

"Mom, I met the ONE!" *Perfect.*

Granny was there in the living room in her chair next to Tina's mom.

"Really, Dearie," Granny excitedly spoke up immediately.

"Now that's BIG, BIG news, isn't it? Who is this lucky "One" fellow?"

Tina could hear every triumphant word from her Granny in the background. "She found the ONE, didn't she? Just like I said, let her go and she'll find her wings. That's what I've said all along!" Granny's cane spilled to the floor. She was dancing and melting the carpet with her quick step.

"Shush, Ma. Shush!" said Tina's mom.

Granny yelled, "Put her on the speaker."

"Hi, Granny. I – I – I kind of found a guy. He's nice and smart. But he's a little older," Tina said.

"What's this about a new job?" Tina's mom talked over Tina's grandmother.

Tina thought to herself, *that's good. Let's get on to talking about the job.*

41

Good Trouble Finds Tina and Enrique

Tina had yet to level completely with her mom. Tina wanted her mom's approval. It wasn't a deal breaker. Tina had made up her mind. Maybe she shouldn't have, but this opportunity was too good to be true. Enrique's offer was a dream job—with travel, writing, excitement, responsibility, and Enrique.

Enrique would do everything he could to make Tina's job as his assistant attractive. He hoped she would commit to the team when she realized the opportunity. She had fierce determination. She could handle pressure and knew how to use a firearm. He laughed to himself at the thought.

Tina was a great communicator, and she had wherewithal. With Tina at his side, he was free to focus on team building and succession planning.

As far as Enrique was concerned, you could dash all the other "intelligences." Wherewithal was paramount. It was the ability to get the right information, prioritize it, then build, communicate, and enact an action plan, and finally, keep it all in perspective. Wherewithal was his calling card, his family's calling card, and his drive and focus. Wherewithal determined their success!

He hadn't told Tina all his plans. It was too much too soon. Robert (his son) wanted to expand the business. Robert felt the service and operations side of their business was strong. It was. It had Enrique's no-nonsense "stamp" all over it. *Don't expect what you don't inspect.*

Robert and his team were working on honing the message of the Mistresses of the Sea brand. In Robert's view, marketing was their company's weakness. Their competition, whose services weren't half as good, splashed enticing ads in the media continually while their own marketing group seemed unable to perfect the best message to reach their target audience.

When Enrique and Robert spoke several months earlier, Robert planted the seed with Enrique for romance to be the centerpiece of their marketing campaign. How ironic for Enrique to be involved in exactly the type of romance his son hoped would spark their business.

Enrique wondered what Robert would think about him and Tina. Their romance had struck lightning quick in the middle of Enrique's company initiative for succession planning for the entire fleet staff.

Wherewithal had driven all of his successful decisions. Enrique remembered one summer as a young boy when his dad brought him on an overnight hunting trip. Surprisingly, his dad hadn't instructed Enrique about what to bring for the trip.

After an arduous five-hour hike into the mountains near their home, Enrique asked his dad for something to eat. His dad asked him, "What did you bring Enrique?"

"Nothing, Papa."

Enrique hadn't packed a sandwich or fruit or anything. Enrique Sr. had prepared Enrique's Mom not to intervene. She wasn't happy, but she went along with her husband's wishes. The boy needed to learn.

"You are on your own, son." His Dad chewed on a small piece of jerky. As night fell, there was no game to shoot—no turkeys, no deer, not even a squirrel crossed their path. They went to sleep hungry. Neither of them brought a fishing rod—just hunting rifles. After a restless sleep, they awoke to birds chirping and owls hooting. Enrique's dad didn't ask him if he was hungry. Instead, Enrique's dad asked, "What are the deer eating today? Are they hungry?"

Enrique decided to look for fruits and berries and anything he could find. He found a few berry bushes and some flowers he remembered were edible. Not much was said between him and his father on the long walk home.

Planning would become Enrique's priority. His father had had helped build their family business with "magical" moments like their "no catch" hunting trip. Wherewithal was the end goal. Tina had wherewithal. All of his top hires had wherewithal and proved it on a regular basis.

Tina went back and forth on what part to tell her mom first. She thought her Mom would generally think the news was good.

But her Mom was just getting used to Tina's freelance job status as a writer. Enrique's age was another hurdle.

Tina had already decided to take the job with the Arnoldo family business. Enrique was offering her an unbeatable opportunity. It was her dream job.

Half-way through the SXM flight, they were holding hands like teenagers on a first date. She smiled to herself when she looked at him. She was almost ready to ask him, but it just didn't seem the right time to ask, "How old are you anyways?" It seemed comical to even ask.

Their plane descended skillfully down from 5,000 feet toward the short runway in St. Maarten. They breezed over the "Sunset Beach Bar" near the Maho Hotel. The bar sat above a tiny outcropping of rip-rap stone that had been installed to protect the bar. The rip-rap didn't offer the protection of a seawall, but it served to protect the bar at high tide from smaller storms. Tourists flocked to that beach and the bar to see other carefree souls get pushed into the water by forceful airstreams from the incoming jets' low trajectories.

When their plane arrived in the terminal, a ship porter and taxi awaited them with a sign that said, "Arnoldo Group – 2."

Enrique said, "Hi Max. How is it going?"

Max, responded: "It's all good, Chief. Good to see you back with us again. Captain Jillean will be pleased too. Will you be staying on board "The Splendid Romance," or at the company condo?"

"Take us to the ship first. Let's get a handle on this cable issue.

"Got it, Chief."

They sped off only to be stoppd in traffic right away. Philipsburg was only nine kilometers from Princess Juliana airport, but the traffic was horrendous. Max weaved his way through a few short-cuts and soon they pulled up to the dock where "The Splendid Romance" was moored.

"Thanks, Max," Enrique shouted as he grabbed his small tote and ran to gangplank. Tina wasn't far behind. He walked at a brisk pace. She matched his every step.

"Max," he shouted over his shoulder. "Get the luggage to the condo. I don't know how long we'll be, but we'll find our way over later."

"Yes, sir," Max replied.

Captain Jillean was waiting. "Hi, Enrique. Hi, Tina. Come on up to the bridge so you can have a look at the underwater camera footage."

Tina was impressed. Everyone in the company was no-nonsense."

In just minutes they viewed the camera footage. Enrique pointed at the cable end and said, "Jillean, look at the rusty build-up on that twisted cable end. It's been sheared off for some time. I've seen that configuration before. I think it's a continental company cable. If we cut the lower housing, it should give us the manufacturer and maybe we can trace it back to the installer. If we can do that, we can send a repair dispatch directly to them. With that info we can notify the harbormaster that the port floor is safe."

"Okay," replied Captain Jillean. "The water is clear right now, and with the daylight we should be able to get it done quickly. I'll have the dive team get on it."

Tina decided to study the footage more carefully to identify any risks. She noticed what appeared to be two black handles partly buried in the sand. She pointed them out to Enrique on the screen.

Enrique said, "Magnify that angle. Those look like bolt cutters. I'll be damned. What the hell? I think someone might have intentionally cut this piece loose."

Enrique continued, "Let's ease off on talking to the harbormaster just yet. I'll go on the dive to see for myself."

"Not without me," Tina quickly insisted.

Enrique smiled. Tina was everything he expected and more.

They were in forty feet of warm water. They suited up with masks, air tanks, fins, and bags. They didn't need wetsuits. Tina moved fluidly through the water like a fish. Enrique was a dive master with hundreds of dives under his belt. Ten minutes into their dive, they had retrieved a set of bolt cutters from under the cable end.

Now there were new questions to be answered. Were the bolt cutters a simple lost tool from a work crew, or was there something more sinister at work? It mattered, especially for the expansion of the Arnoldo Fleet. What roles did Enrique plan for each member of the team? How would he shape that effort?

42

New and Young Blood to Re-Build the Fleet

E nrique, Tina, and the dive team examined the bolt cutters up on the deck. The dive team was perplexed. Perhaps the abandoned cutters were a coincidence. Perhaps someone had dropped their bolt cutters in the turbulence while working to free up the cable end but forgot to report the incident.

Enrique looked at Tina and said, "Tina, let's wrap this up. I have enough information. He did not want to seem overly worried. Please get the memo over to the harbormaster. We have a boat to purchase in Holland. That's our next stop.

Tina was finishing the "Delay Memo:"

Dear Passengers:

Regrettably we must endure an overnight in St. Maarten before we can safely continue our cruise. The cable restoration will be complete in the morning. Enjoy an additional ten percent discount on all purchases this evening. Our cruise will restart at 0600 hours.

Enrique gave Tina's memo a quick review. He noted her initiative in offering the discount. Tina had the good instincts of a smart businesswoman.

Tina asked him, "What is the name of the new ship?"

Enrique said, "We haven't decided yet. We know we need young ideas and new blood. I'm thinking 'Fresh Romance for All.'"

Tina shot back to him, "Let's call her 'The Romantic Seas.' We'll get a couples guru to give seminars onboard the maiden voyage. I'll put together some brochure bullet points."

Enrique liked what he heard. Enrique felt like Tina was writing the Arnoldo Company's next chapter.

Maybe she was. He encouraged Tina to write a romance novel to celebrate the Arnoldo's new direction and their newest ship. He knew she'd be successful.

Acknowledgements

It takes a village to write a book; I live in the finest of villages.

To all who have helped me traverse a trail I never imagined riding.

My deepest appreciation for my wife and family—true saints, angels, and heroes in my life—along with my Publishing teams at One Stop Publishing (Meredith Dunn, Charissa Newell, Erin Hemme Froslie, Serena Finochio, and Elle Dubois) and The Book Professionals (Jay Cooper, Ben Andrews, and Maurice Strauss).

I offer sincere gratitude to our editing guru Meredith Dunn, an expert in just the right amount of pressure a writer needs to stay the course and win the writing battle. She is an inspiration for excellence!

Special thanks to my KC Team—Dave Kelley, Lisa Flashenburg, Gaby Tueme, Rina and Flavio Silva, Dave Mullen, Sam Reef, and Dave Flashenburg. How lucky I am!

A GIANT thank you to the people who enable me to seize each day with vigor. To my doctors and nurses, and medical teams in the background who've kept me alive through Cancer(s), Pneumonia(s), heart issues, diseases, and multiple broken bones: Dr. Yakov Weinreb, Dr. Lakshmi Nayak, Dr. Andrew Kriegel, Dr. Mazen Eneyni, Dr. Peter Schnoor, Dr. Lindsay Emminger,

Dr. Jarod Santoro, Dr. Timothy Smith, and Dr. Ann LaCasce all deserve special recognition for helping me stay healthy to live life the fullest every day.

Sincere thanks to my mountain biking teams who continue to support my journeys on the trails, in writing, and in life: Luis, Steven, Anthony, Malcolm, Jason, Luke, Gary, Fast Rob, Matty, Chowe, Aya, Deb, Harley, Drew, Ross, Steve M., Dave R., Guy, Manny, Steve, Joe, Dalton, Keri, Arnoldo, Carlos, Tony, Tom, George, Dave, Jim, Chris, Matt, Mark, Shawn, Vanessa, Kevin, Karen, Mark, and the whole Bike Barn team.

We all need supporters, and mine are exceptional: Brad Durant, John Howe, Ken Ryvicker, Jorge Cardoso, Robert Luckock, Carol McAdoo Rehme, Joe Feaster, Lynne and Randy Barker, Pat and Jerry Gautreau, Alan Lury, Becky and Dennis Devlin, Sam Reef, Bob Mendillo, Lenny Love, Sarah Feragen, Eric Dias, James and Yola Thorp, Grace and Pat Fitzpatrick, Gene Sperry, Max Essex, Dan Juliani, Chris Carlow, Owen McElroy, Mark Terry, and Scot Robison—one of the best!

As always, special thanks to my mentors: Ed Ostrander (who is alive in every story we tell) and his beautiful wife Linda Ostrander, who together continue their inspiration in my life.

HOW LUCKY I AM!

2022 Next Generation Indie Book Awards Finalist

Memoirs (Personal Struggle/ Health Issues)

AWARDED TO:

Cancer R.I.P.: The Ultimate Fight

"Steve Kelley's *Cancer R.I.P.* is an invaluable window for all physicians to see how one extraordinary patient personally perceives his cancer and the emotional toll of our treatments on him. Written with wit, wisdom, and thoroughly entertaining prose, *Cancer R.I.P.* is a beautiful lesson to both patient and physician."

— YAKOV KOGAN, M.D.